"I never thought you were the type to play with fire, Maggie."

She chuckled softly, her heart racing now in response to that all-too-brief kiss. "I've been known to scorch my fingertips a few times."

His hands settled at her hips before she could move away. "My fingers are still feeling a little cold."

What the hell. She wrapped her arms around his neck, momentarily abandoning caution. "Then maybe we should heat them up."

"Maybe we should." He settled his mouth against hers, their smiles meeting then melding into a kiss hot enough to scorch much more than her fingertips. She felt the heat surging all the way through her, simmering deep inside her. This buttoned-down, ex-military single dad definitely knew how to kiss.

A MATCH FOR THE SINGLE DAD

BY
GINA WILKINS

First published in Great Britain 2013
by Mills & Boon, an imprint of Harlequin (UK) Limited,
Eton House, 18-24 Paradise Road, Richmond, Surrey TW9 1SR

© Gina Wilkins 2013

ISBN: 978 0 263 90127 6
ebook ISBN: 978 1 472 00507 6

23-0713

Harlequin (UK) policy is to use papers that are natural, renewable and recyclable products and made from wood grown in sustainable forests. The logging and manufacturing processes conform to the legal environmental regulations of the country of origin.

Printed and bound in Spain
by Blackprint CPI, Barcelona

Gina Wilkins is a bestselling and award-winning author who has written more than seventy novels for Mills & Boon. She credits her successful career in romance to her long, happy marriage and her three "extraordinary" children.

A lifelong resident of central Arkansas, Ms Wilkins sold her first book to Mills & Boon in 1988 and has been writing full-time since. She has appeared on the Waldenbooks, B. Dalton and *USA TODAY* bestseller lists. She is a three-time recipient of a Maggie Award for Excellence, sponsored by Georgia Romance Writers, and has won several awards from the reviewers of *RT Book Reviews*.

For Patience Bloom, a dedicated editor,
fellow romance fan and genuinely nice person.

Chapter One

"He'll say no. Daddy always says no," almost-eleven-year-old Kristina McHale said glumly. She was known to her family and friends as Kix, a nickname bestowed on her by her slightly older sister, Payton, who'd had trouble as a toddler saying her baby sister's formal name.

With the wisdom of her thirteen years, Payton waved a hand dismissively. "We can talk him into it. You know how he's always nagging about 'family time.' Well, a week together in a cabin would count for that, right? Besides, that week includes both your birthday and the Fourth of July. How can he say no?"

"He'll find a way," Kix predicted.

Payton sighed in response to her sister's pessimism. "We can at least ask. *You* ask. Give him the look. You know, puppy-dog eyes. I'll act like I think it's sort of a dumb idea, so he won't figure out we're conspirators."

"Con—cons—?"

"Working together," Payton explained impatiently.

"Oh." Kix practiced widening her already-big blue eyes. "You think this will help?"

Eyeing her critically, Payton shrugged. "Couldn't hurt. Lower your chin a little and maybe poke out your bottom lip. If you could make it kind of quiver a little, it would be even better."

"Like this?" Kix gave her sister a limpid look from beneath thick dark lashes, her rosy mouth pursed in a hint of a pout.

"Not bad. I bet he'll say yes. Once we have him at the resort for a whole week, we'll make sure he spends time with her."

"How are we going to do that?"

Payton sighed impatiently and pushed an auburn strand out of her face. "I can't think of everything all at once, Kix. We just will, okay?"

"Okay."

Pacing the length of her bedroom, Payton continued her scheming. "Once Dad spends more time with Maggie, surely he'll get around to asking her out. I mean, we know he likes her because he always smiles when she's around, right?"

Sitting cross-legged on her sister's bed, Kix nodded enthusiastically, her brighter-red hair tumbling into her freckled face. "He has to like her. He'd be crazy if he didn't."

"Well, it *is* Dad," Payton muttered, making Kix giggle. "Still, maybe he'll finally do something right and ask her out. And maybe we'll finally have someone on our side for a change who'll tell Dad he has to stop treating us like dumb little girls. Maggie always looks so pretty. I bet she'd convince Dad and Grammy that we're old enough for makeup and double-pierced ears and cool clothes. At least, I am."

"Hey!"

"Well, you're almost old enough," Payton conceded. "And there are other things she could take your side about."

"Yeah, I guess."

"So we're agreed? You'll tell him tonight at dinner that you know where you want to spend your birthday week?"

"Agreed."

They exchanged a complicated handshake to seal the deal.

Early on a Sunday morning in June, Maggie Bell shifted on the wooden picnic table bench beneath the big pavilion at Bell Resort and Marina. The newly risen sun glittered on the rippling waters of southeast Texas's Lake Livingston ahead, making the lake look like liquid silver streaked with veins of gold. Even this early, the air was already quite warm, though she was comfortable enough in her scoop-neck, cap-sleeve yellow T-shirt dress and wedge-heeled sandals.

Seated around her at long wooden picnic tables and in folding chairs beneath the big pavilion at Bell Resort and Marina, a small crowd sang the chorus of "Amazing Grace," most of them even in the same key. In a long-standing tradition at the resort owned by Maggie's family, nondenominational sunrise worship services were held year-round for guests and any area residents who chose to participate. Attendance had always been good, but especially during the past few months. Specifically, since good-looking and personable Jasper Bettencourt had started leading the services.

Golden-haired, blue-eyed, male-model handsome, always casually dressed in jeans and cotton shirts, Jasper, known to his friends as Jay, hardly fit the stereotype of a small-town minister. Longtime locals remembered him as a hell-raising teen from a dysfunctional family who had escaped the area more than fifteen years before. It had been quite a shock when he'd returned with a theology degree, founded a little nondenominational church and dedicated himself to community service and caring for the aging, former-pastor uncle who was his only living relative. He was a compelling speaker, a talented singer and a genuinely nice guy who drew people to him with his mix of humor, kindness and compassion. Each Sunday he led the sunrise service attendees in a few well-known hymns, accompanied on guitar by his friend Garrett McHale, before presenting a brief but always moving sermon.

Seated in a folding chair beneath the pavilion with the morning's printed program gripped loosely in her hands, Maggie sang the familiar song without needing to refer to the lyrics. She chose instead to watch the accompanist.

Dressed in a green shirt and neatly pressed khakis, Garrett looked like the ex-Air Force officer he was. Tall and lean, he wore his brown hair in a crisp, short cut that emphasized the few gray strands at his temples. His posture was impeccable, his movements measured and efficient. His eyes were the same clear gray-blue as the early-morning sky. Garrett, too, had grown up in this area, leaving to join the military at about the same time his lifelong best buddy, Jay, had struck off for parts unknown. Garrett wasn't as strikingly handsome as Jay, yet for some reason Maggie's attention was always drawn to him. She wasn't sure of his exact age, but she'd guess he was maybe ten or eleven years older than her own twenty-seven. The age difference didn't bother her. The fact that he was a single dad to two girls just heading into their teens was a different matter altogether.

She glanced at the auburn-haired thirteen-year-old at her left, then at the almost-eleven-year-old redhead on her right. Garrett's daughters, Payton and Kix, always sat near her during services. A few months ago, she'd filled in part-time for a few weeks at the local country club for a tennis instructor recuperating from emergency surgery. She'd gotten to know Payton and Kix in the kids' class. She was hardly a tennis pro, but the club owner was a family friend who'd been in a bind and who knew Maggie had played competitively during high school and college. Somehow, Maggie had allowed herself to be persuaded to fill in.

At about the same time Maggie had taught his daughters, Garrett had started joining his friend Jay for Sunday sunrise services, bringing Maggie and his girls together even more often. She was fond of both Payton and Kix, but they were a handful. She couldn't imagine being responsible for their full-time care and well-being.

Jay closed the meeting with a prayer and an open invitation to the little church in town where he would hold services later that morning. He made himself available to shake hands and speak with guests afterward while Garrett packed away his acoustic guitar. Payton and Kix started chattering the moment the service ended, telling her about their activities since they'd seen her last Sunday, talking over each other in attempts to claim her full attention.

"…and I love your red leather sandals with the cork

wedge heels so much, but Dad won't let me even look at heels yet because he says they aren't *practical* for someone my age…"

"…and my friend Kimmy got her own smartphone, but Daddy says no way can I have one…"

"…and there was a really great party at Nikea's house, but of course Dad wouldn't let me go just because most of the kids were older than me…"

"…and I wanted to play video games with my friend but Grammy made me clean my room, and it could have waited until later, but she…"

Laughing, Maggie held up both hands. "Girls, girls! I can only listen to one of you at a time."

They started again without noticeable success in being patient, but Maggie managed to follow along for the most part. A litany of complaints about their father was not-so-well buried in their babbling. She had already observed that he ran a fairly strict household, though it was obvious—to her, at least—that he was crazy about his girls. She suspected he was simply overwhelmed at times. His only assistance in raising them came from his mother and grandmother, who shared a house on the same block as the one in which Garrett lived with his daughters. From what little she had seen of the family, it seemed as though Garrett was almost as responsible for the older women as he was for his daughters.

This was a man encumbered by serious baggage.

Guitar case in hand, he approached with a faint smile. Why did she find the slight curve of his firm lips so much more appealing than Jay's bright, beaming grins? She liked Jay very much, but there was just something about Garrett….

"Good morning, Maggie," he said in his deep voice that never failed to elicit a shiver of reaction from her.

She liked to believe she'd become an expert at hiding that response behind a breezy smile. "Good morning, Garrett. The music was especially nice today."

"I just play some chords," he said with a little shrug. "Jay chooses the songs. But I'm glad you enjoyed it."

"I was just going to tell her about my birthday plans, Daddy," Kix said, bouncing up and down on her white sandals. "I'm so excited!"

Maggie smiled indulgently at the littlest McHale sister. As she almost always did, Kix wore her favorite pink, which clashed cheerfully with her flame-red hair but looked just right, somehow, on the adorable girl. "Sounds intriguing. What's the plan, Kix?"

"We're coming *here*," Kix almost shouted in reply. "For a whole week! Isn't that *sweet*?"

"Not quite a week," her father corrected. "Monday afternoon through Sunday service."

Kix waved off those details as unimportant. "Daddy rented a cabin and we're coming a week from tomorrow. My birthday is that Tuesday and we're going to have a party in the cabin—and you can come! And Grammy and Meemaw are coming, too. And we're going swimming and fishing and hiking and boating and Daddy's going to take the whole week off work and we'll make s'mores and—"

"Kix," her father interrupted firmly, "take a breath."

"I hadn't heard you were coming," Maggie said in the brief ensuing lull. She wondered why the information shook her a little. After all, she saw Garrett—er, the McHale family—every Sunday, so why did the thought of him—er, them—being here every day for almost a week throw off her usual equilibrium?

"Kix just sprang this request on me last week," Garrett admitted. "I was actually surprised a cabin was available on such short notice, especially considering it's the Fourth of July week. I told Kix I couldn't promise anything, but fortunately for us there was a late cancellation, so we were able to grab the reservation."

"I'm glad we could accommodate you," Maggie said automatically, then glanced at Kix. "So you wanted to spend your birthday week here, so close to home?"

"*I* wanted to go to the beach." Payton looked and sounded utterly bored. "Like Padre Island or somewhere cool. But no, Kix had to come here where we come every single Sunday. Lame, huh?"

"But, Payton— Ouch!"

"Payton, did you just punch your sister?" Garrett demanded sternly.

"No, Daddy," Kix assured him, innocently wide-eyed as she not-so-surreptitiously rubbed her arm. "She just sort of bumped into me."

"There's a bunch of geese swimming by the pier," Payton said quickly. "Can I take Kix down to look at them?"

He hesitated a moment, then nodded. "Don't get too close to the water. And we can't stay long. I have things to do today."

"You can talk to Maggie while we look at the geese," Payton told him before turning to dash toward the lake with her sister.

Something in the teen's voice made Maggie blink a couple of times. Surely Payton wasn't trying her hand at matchmaking? But Garrett didn't react, so she told herself she must have misunderstood. After all, why would Payton want yet another adult in her already oversupervised—according to her, at least—life?

"How have you been, Maggie?" he asked politely when they were alone.

"Fine, thank you," she replied, equally cordial. "And you?"

He shrugged. "Busy. But fine."

She knew that in addition to taking care of his daughters, his mother and his grandmother, Garrett taught flying lessons and piloted charter flights out of the small local airport. During the past few months, Payton and Kix had told her he'd left the military, in which he'd most recently served as a flight instructor at Laughlin Air Force Base, after the unexpected death a little more than a year ago of their mother, his ex-wife. He had moved back to this area to be closer to his mother and grandmother.

Garrett and the girls' mother had divorced when Kix was only a baby. They had shared custody afterward, though the girls had lived primarily with their mother. Their home with her had been in San Antonio, a three-hour drive from the base, so they'd seen their father on alternate weekends and holidays for the most part, which had meant a huge adjustment for all of them when he'd become solely responsible for them.

In listening to the girls chatter about their lives, Maggie had gotten the impression that they had loved their mother but had spent as much time with nannies and babysitters as with her. "She was gone a lot," Payton had said simply. "She was a lawyer, so she worked long hours and she had lots of professional clubs and parties and stuff she had to go to most evenings. She liked to hang out with her friends on weekends, because she said she worked so hard during the week that she needed down time."

Time away from her children, Maggie had interpreted in a knee-jerk reaction of disapproval she'd tried to suppress. She told herself she had no right to judge a woman she'd never even met based on perhaps-exaggerated stories from two children.

"Maybe you need a vacation as much as the girls do," she suggested to Garrett. "We'll try to make sure you have a good time while you're here."

She spoke, of course, as a representative of the resort. No personal messages intended.

"Thank you," he said.

She cleared her throat silently. Darn, but this man made her teeth tingle. How very inconvenient of him.

"So, um, your grandmother is coming with you for the week?" she asked with a lift of her eyebrows.

His smile turned rueful. "She is. She doesn't want to be left out, even though she has given me an earful about how she'll be spending six days in enemy territory."

Maggie couldn't help laughing. Her grandmother, Dixie Bell, and his, Esther Lincoln, were lifelong rivals who saw each other as mortal enemies. It had begun back when they were in junior high competing for the attentions of the same boys, though Esther was a year ahead in school. The rivalry had continued when they participated in county-fair cooking contests after they'd married, competing for blue ribbons and each bitterly accusing the other of underhandedness.

"I'm sure Mimi will be a gracious host," she said, mentally crossing her fingers. "They probably won't see each other much, anyway. Mimi's usually in the offices or the store."

"I've already told Meemaw that she has to be polite while she's here," Garrett replied with a chuckle.

She found it incredibly appealing to hear this serious-natured, somewhat stern-looking ex-military officer talk about his "Meemaw." But then, she found entirely too much appealing about Garrett.

He glanced at his watch. "I'd better collect the girls. I've got some appointments this afternoon. Nice to visit with you as always, Maggie. We'll see you next Sunday morning."

"Actually, I'll be out of town next weekend. I'm visiting my sister in Dallas to spend some time with her and the baby while her husband's at a conference in Chicago. But I'll be back Sunday evening, so I'll be around if your family needs anything during your stay."

Garrett nodded, then looked at her with a bemused expression. "I have to admit Kix's request to spend her birthday week here caught me by surprise. It seemed to come out of the blue. She said she didn't even need another present, just the time here."

"Maybe she just wanted to spend a week with her family without the usual distractions at home," she suggested.

Garrett appeared skeptical. "According to her and Payton, they spend too much time with family as it is. Payton wanted to go to Padre Island for our vacation, but Kix was insistent on coming here, so Payton agreed since it's Kix's birthday."

"That was nice of her."

"Yeah." But she noted that Garrett still seemed perplexed by his daughters' behavior when he bade her goodbye and walked away.

She wished him luck dealing with two girls of that age. It was certainly more responsibility than she'd want to take on.

"Let's go to the playground!" Kix hopped out of the SUV immediately upon arrival at the resort just after noon on the Monday of their vacation week. "C'mon, Payton, let's see who can make it all the way across the monkey bars without falling."

"Whoa. Hold up there." Garrett moved to stand in front of her. "We have a ton of stuff to carry inside, and you're helping."

"Okay," she said cheerfully enough, changing course to head for the back of the vehicle. "We can go to the playground later."

"Don't you be running off without permission or supervision," Garrett's mom fussed to Kix. Sixty-year-old Paulette Lincoln McHale was medium height, broad-shouldered and hipped, with crisp gray hair and strong features. Yet despite her sturdy, rather imposing appearance, she was a compulsive worrier who tended to hover over the girls. "There are strangers in the camp-grounds and the motel and the other cabins. One of us adults will need to go with you when you wander around the resort, you hear?"

Garrett watched as his daughters swapped exasperated looks and heaved long-suffering sighs before loading their arms with bags to carry inside the cabin.

Eighty-one-year-old Esther Lincoln, known in the family as Meemaw, was stronger than her daughter emotionally, though her body was going frail. Her hair was a cap of bright white curls around her soft face. Her shoulders were stooped and she relied on a walker to steady her gait, but her fiery spirit was undimmed. "Let the girls have some fun, Paulette. They're not going to run wild around the place, and they know to be careful."

"You can't be too careful these days," Garrett's mother retorted darkly.

Garrett juggled two suitcases and a bag of groceries he'd removed from the well-packed vehicle. "Let's just take the stuff inside and then we'll make plans."

Though it bore the number six, the cabin to which they'd been assigned sat in the center of five lakeside rentals numbered four through eight. The cabins ranged in size from the little one-bedroom A-frames at each end of the row to the four-bedroom cottage where Garrett's family would spend the next six days. A long, welcoming front porch held rockers and a swing. Inside, the living area, kitchen and dining nook made up the open central floor plan. There was a separate bedroom for each adult and a sleeping loft for the girls to share. A big back deck furnished with wrought-iron tables and chairs invited guests to sit and admire the lake.

Kix looked forward to gathering around the fire pit in the evening to roast hot dogs and marshmallows, both of which Garrett had brought along. Between the groceries he'd purchased and the home-cooked goodies his mother and grandmother had insisted on preparing and bringing along, they probably had enough food for at least twice as many days as he'd booked for their stay.

He insisted the girls help put everything away before they played. He'd already launched the boat he'd towed behind the SUV, secured it into a slip he'd rented for the week and parked the trailer in the provided lot near the marina. The lot had been crowded; even this early in the holiday week, business was brisk at the resort.

He'd owned the fish-and-ski boat for several years. The girls always liked going out in it, one of the few things they seemed to enjoy doing with him these days. When their mother was alive, he'd spent many of his custody weekends taking them boating on waters near the base. They hadn't considered him quite so lame back then, he thought regretfully. Probably due to a combination of them being younger and seeing him more rarely, making him less of a constant authority figure to be rebelled against.

Breanne had been more indulgent with them, spoiling them with material possessions to assuage her guilt for spending so little time with them. She hadn't been a bad mother, just a distracted one. Breanne had been easily bored. Most especially with him.

Shaking off thoughts of his late ex-wife—and what had brought her to mind, anyway?—he nodded in approval when the girls reported that their things were all stowed away upstairs.

"Okay, what's on the agenda?" he asked, having promised to leave the activities for the week to them—within reason.

Kix bounced around him. "We want to go out in the boat and have milk shakes at the diner and hike through the resort and play board games and cook hot dogs and—"

"Breathe, Kix."

She giggled.

"Let's go find Maggie and see if she wants to go out in the boat with us," Payton suggested.

Both the girls had expressed disappointment that they hadn't yet seen Maggie. A resort employee introducing herself as Rosie had checked them in at the main desk, and Maggie's uncle, C. J. Bell, had assisted with the boat launch and slip parking at the marina. They had seen a few other faces familiar from Sunday services and Saturday boating-and-swimming visits to the resort, but there'd been no sight of Maggie.

"Maggie is working now," he told his daughters firmly. "Remember you both promised not to bother her."

Kix frowned in dissatisfaction. "She owns the resort. Can't she take off when she wants to?"

"Her family owns the resort, and Maggie takes her responsibilities seriously," he chided. "Just as you can't ditch school whenever you want, Maggie can't just stop her work."

"Let's go for a walk down by the water," Garrett's mother suggested. "I think I saw some ducks."

Kix was already moving toward the door. "They're geese, Grammy. Canada geese. There's a whole flock of them who live here."

"It's a gaggle, not a flock," Payton corrected her, heading more slowly toward the back door.

"Y'all go on for your walk, I'm going to sit here and rest awhile," Garrett's grandmother announced, lowering herself into an armchair. "Garrett, honey, hand me my yarn bag, please. Payton, sweetie, be a lamb and fetch Meemaw a bottle of that strawberry-flavored water we brought along."

Because the chair looked comfortable and faced a nice view of the lake, Garrett figured his grandmother had found her roost for the duration of the vacation. She would be perfectly content to sit right there and be waited on hand and foot for the next five and a half days, though he and his mother would nag her into getting at least a minimum of exercise, as her doctors recommended.

"Are you coming with us on our walk, Daddy?" Kix asked from the back door.

"I'm going out to make sure we got everything from the car. I'll catch up with you in a little while."

"Tie your shoelaces, Kix," he heard his mother say before the door closed behind the trio. "You'll trip over them if they're loose."

A green utility golf cart emblazoned with the resort logo pulled into the driveway behind Garrett's vehicle just as he was checking the door locks. He smiled when he saw Maggie at the wheel. Her thick, sun-streaked brown hair, a little tousled from the drive in the open cart, fell loose to her shoulders, framing her pretty face. She wore a short-sleeved lavender top with a deep scoop neck that just flirted with a tasteful hint of cleavage. Jeans and brown leather wedge-heeled sandals completed her casual outfit. She seemed to favor wedge heels, and he had to admit they did great things for her long legs. As she slid out of the cart, Garrett wondered how she managed to look so sleek and put-together even in casual clothing suitable for her work.

"Hi, Garrett. Are you all settled in?" she asked, leaning against the front of the cart. "Is there anything you need?"

He'd heard some say that Maggie's older sister, Hannah, was the beauty of the Bell family with her dark hair and emerald eyes and near-perfect features. He'd met Hannah a couple of times and agreed that she was lovely. But there was something about Maggie, with her clear hazel eyes and not-quite-so-perfect face, her pleasant smiles and friendly manner. She radiated competence and efficiency, projecting a quiet calmness in the middle of occasional chaos. With his own life so often in uproar, he appreciated the serenity that seemed to surround Maggie.

She was too young for him, of course—at least a decade younger—though he had to remind himself of that fact often when he was with her. Of course he was attracted to her—what red-blooded single man wouldn't be?—but he had no intention of doing anything about it. He doubted that a woman her age would be interested in an older man with his heavy responsibilities. Especially a man who'd been divorced by his wife because she found him too boring to make their relationship worth the effort required.

He didn't think of himself as boring, but he could understand how his enhanced sense of duty—to his family, his job, his country—made him less appealing to someone who thrived on spontaneity and self-indulgence. Not that Maggie seemed to be that type, but being young, pretty and single, she was certainly free to live on impulse if she wanted. Unlike himself.

"We don't need anything, but thanks for asking." He patted the closed tailgate of his SUV. "I'm pretty sure my family would have brought along everything they own if I hadn't set limits. You wouldn't believe how full this thing was, especially considering we're less than fifteen miles from home."

She laughed. "I never mastered the art of packing light. My dad used to fuss whenever we loaded the car to go anywhere."

Leaning back against his vehicle, he crossed his arms casually over his chest. "So where do resort owners go for vacation?"

She smiled ruefully. "Mostly we went to visit family in Shreveport and Tulsa. A few times we drove down to Galveston to stay in a beach cabin, and once we went to the mountains in Colorado. With a family-owned business, it isn't easy to get away for vacations. We had to trade off weeks with my uncle's family, usually during off-season here at the resort."

During the past months, Garrett had learned that the Bell Resort and Marina had been founded by Maggie's grandparents, Carl and Dixie Bell, on land previously owned by Carl's parents. Carl and Dixie's sons, Carl Jr.

and Bryan, along with their wives, Sarah and Linda, had worked alongside their parents to build the resort into a successful vacation destination. Each member of the family had taken on a particular area of operation according to his or her personal interests. Carl Jr. ran the marina, his wife worked the grill, Bryan was responsible for grounds and maintenance and Linda ran the convenience store. Full-time and part-time employees were hired from outside to work the check-in desk, man the front gate and assist in other areas as needed.

Carl Jr.—nicknamed C.J.—and Sarah had three children, Steven, Shelby and Lori. Steven had worked for the resort until recently, when he'd left to fulfill his lifelong dream and train as a firefighter. Lori had quit college and eloped with a musician early in the summer, to the shock of her entire family. Of those siblings, only Shelby, a C.P.A. and business manager for the resort, was still fully committed to the family business, along with her new husband, Aaron Walker, who'd taken on Steven's responsibilities helping Bryan keep up the grounds and supervise part-time seasonal workers hired to assist them.

Bryan and Linda's two daughters, Hannah and Maggie, still worked for the resort, though Hannah, who handled marketing, now telecommuted from the home in Dallas she shared with her husband, Aaron Walker's twin brother, Andrew, and their baby daughter. From what Garrett had deduced, Maggie was in charge of hiring and supervising the housekeeping staff for the cabins and the sixteen-unit motel on the grounds.

It was all very efficient, as far as he could tell. The family seemed to get along quite well, considering they lived and worked in such close quarters—Lori's rebellion notwithstanding. Yet he wondered if Maggie ever felt the urge to try her hand at a different career, like Steven, or take off on a reckless adventure, like Lori. No one understood better than he the constraints of family obligation, even when those shackles were donned willingly.

"Be sure and let us know if there's anything at all you need during your stay with us," Maggie said, every inch the gracious hostess.

She tossed back a lock of hair that a playful breeze swept into her face and Garrett felt his chest tighten. She really was attractive. He'd bet her thick, shoulder-length, gold-streaked brown hair felt as soft as it looked. Not to mention her silky, peach-dusted skin....

He cleared his throat. Hard. He'd neglected his social life badly during the past year, since he'd left the Air Force and become responsible for his girls. He really should find time to date again—though that would involve actually meeting someone he wanted to go out with. Present company excluded, of course.

She pulled a card from her pocket and extended it to him. "This is my cell phone number if you need to contact me. I'm not aware of any maintenance issues with your cabin, but if you have any problems, just give me a call and I'll send someone immediately."

Their fingers brushed when he accepted the card. He blamed static in the air for the resulting ripple of awareness, though there hadn't actually been a shock.

"Thanks," he said, drawing his hand away to tuck the card in his back jeans pocket.

"So, I'll see you around."

"Yeah, about that. We're having a birthday cake for Kix at about seven tomorrow evening. She'd love it if you joined us."

Though they'd met most of the Bell family in passing, the girls were particularly attached to Maggie because of the tennis classes she'd taught them. Neither of his daughters seemed to have a particular affinity for the sport, but they'd certainly taken to their instructor. Couldn't say he blamed them for that.

"I'd be happy to join you for cake," Maggie said with a bright smile. "Can I bring anything?"

"Trust me, we have more than enough. For that matter, you can bring your whole family and there would still be enough."

She laughed. "I'll see you tomorrow, then. Enjoy your evening."

"I'll certainly try," he murmured, watching her buzz away in the cart, her hair waving lightly around her shoulders. He suspected that image would linger in his mind for a few hours tonight.

Chapter Two

Carrying a large box of red, white and blue decorations she'd retrieved from an upstairs storage room, Maggie descended the stairs carefully into the lobby of the main building later Monday afternoon. She could have used the small elevator they'd installed last year for her grandparents, but it was such a habit to take the stairs that she'd started down without considering how much the box limited her vision. She was almost to the bottom when she missed a step with her foot. Had her reflexes not been quicker, she might well have taken a tumble.

Someone took the box from her hands from below. She blinked in surprise when she saw Garrett standing there, frowning. Even his stern expression looked too darned appealing for her peace of mind, never mind what his rare full smiles did to her.

"You very nearly fell," he chided, bringing her attention back to the moment.

"Guess I got in a hurry," she replied, "but I caught myself."

"I was prepared to catch you if you didn't."

A sudden image of herself cradled in Garrett's strong arms made her momentarily regret her own quick reflexes.

"Where do you want this?"

Ordering herself to stop being so foolish, she motioned toward the reception desk to her left. "Just set it in the corner behind the desk. We're decorating tomorrow for the holiday weekend and I was just bringing down some of the supplies."

Nodding to Rosie Aguilar, who manned the reception desk most weekdays since Maggie's sister had married and moved to Dallas, Garrett set the big box in a back corner. "Do you have any more to bring down? I can help."

"Thanks, but no. That's the only one for now." She glanced around the lobby, expecting to see members of his family. Though a few guests mingled in the large open room that was decorated with lush greenery, shiny trophy fish mounted on wooden plaques and displays of antique fishing lures, she saw no sign of Garrett's daughters.

The reception desk lay straight ahead of the big double-entry doors. To the right upon entering was the Chimes Grill, done in red-and-chrome vintage diner style, and to the left the convenience store stocked with basic groceries, some prepared foods and fishing and camping supplies. Maggie's aunt Sarah ran the grill, whereas the store was her mom's domain. Neither was particularly busy on this Monday afternoon, though a few early dinner guests were seated in the diner. The back of the main building housed the marina that was her uncle C.J.'s domain, which included a bait shop, marine gas pump, fishing pier, boat slips and fish-cleaning station.

"Where are the girls?"

"Back at the cabin," Garrett replied. "We were getting things ready to grill hamburgers for dinner when I realized that we forgot to bring the buns I bought specifically for this trip. Apparently, they're sitting on the kitchen counter back at my house. I figured it would be easier to come into the store to buy some more rather than to drive back home. I'd just walked in when I saw you almost take the header down the stairs."

She waved a hand toward the glass walls of the convenience store. "We happen to stock a good supply of hamburger and hot dog buns. Mom will help you with whatever you need."

He shook his head in self-recrimination. "Can't believe I forgot the buns I bought. It got a little hectic when we were leaving, with both girls wanting to bring a ridiculous amount of stuff, so I ended up leaving behind something we actually needed."

She smiled. "At least it was something easily replaced."

"Yeah." His gaze seemed to linger for a moment on her mouth. And then he raised his eyes to hers. "If you don't already have plans for dinner, maybe you'd like to join us? The girls would love having you. Kix has been asking about you all day."

She hesitated a moment, reminding herself that she would be seeing the girls for birthday cake the next evening, which should probably be enough interaction with them—but then she heard words pop out of her mouth. "That sounds like fun, if you're sure there's enough."

Garrett laughed, such a nice sound that she wished

she could hear it more often. "Trust me, there will be plenty. My mom doesn't believe in cooking just a small amount of anything."

"Then sure, why not? My book club canceled this evening's meeting, so I'm available. What time?"

"Come now if you're finished for the day," he suggested. "My grandmother likes to eat early, so I'll start cooking the burgers as soon as I'm back at the cabin. Won't take long to have them ready."

"I'll put away a few things and meet you in the store."

Garrett was paying for bags of sesame-seed hamburger buns when she rejoined him. She plucked a jar of organic squash pickles off a shelf to take along, showing it to her mother, who nodded and made a note of the purchase. The pickles were made and distributed by a local grower and were a popular item in the resort store. It was the least Maggie could contribute to the meal, since she didn't have time to make anything.

Garrett had walked from the cabin, but Maggie drove him back in one of the ubiquitous green resort golf carts. "So...book club, huh?" he asked on the way.

She grinned. "Well, it's more girlfriends-getting-together-to-drink-wine-eat-ridiculously-high-calorie-desserts-and-dish-gossip club, but we think 'book club' sounds more intellectual."

Garrett laughed. "Good call."

"Yeah, we thought so."

"What else do you do when you aren't working?"

"I try to make it to the gym a few times a week for Zumba classes, and go out to clubs with friends sometimes on weekends for karaoke or dancing. Single life. You know."

He grimaced wryly. "I hardly remember single life.

Married too young, spent most of my life in the military, now a full-time dad. You know."

She couldn't say she knew his life any more than he did hers. Another reminder of how little they had in common, she told herself somberly.

"I should probably warn you that Payton's mad at me," Garrett mentioned as she parked in the driveway of cabin six. "She was barely speaking to me when I left. Maybe I had an ulterior motive inviting you to join us for dinner. She'll be on her best behavior for you."

Maggie smiled sympathetically. "What did you do to get in trouble with her?"

"She met a couple of teenage brothers hanging around the tennis and basketball court this afternoon. She said their name was Ferguson—Trevor and Drake Ferguson. They started talking while I was shooting hoops with Kix. They invited her to meet them down at the lake tonight to 'look at the stars.'" He made ironic quotation marks with his fingers as he spoke the phrase. "Needless to say, I told her she wasn't meeting a couple of strange boys by herself at night. She hasn't spoken to me since, other than to mutter about how I keep treating her like a baby."

Maggie didn't know all the guests registered at the resort at any particular time, of course, but she was passingly familiar with most of the occupants of the motel and cabins. Especially repeat visitors. "I know the family. Wayne and Melanie Alexander and her sons, Trevor and Drake Ferguson. They're in cabin two, over by the motel. They've stayed with us several times before and they like being close to the pool. As I recall, Trevor is maybe fourteen, Drake a couple years younger, a little younger than Payton, I think."

Garrett nodded to acknowledge her identification.

"Payton thought knowing the boys' names would be all I required to approve of her hanging out with them unsupervised. She was wrong."

"The boys have always seemed reasonably well-behaved, but they aren't supervised very closely. I don't blame you for not wanting her to wander down to the lake with them alone at night."

"Not going to happen. No matter how much she pouts. So maybe having you there tonight will ease the sting some."

"In that case, I'll do my best to cheer her up."

"Hope you have better luck with it than I do."

She smoothed a hand over her breeze-tossed hair. "I have an advantage. I wasn't the one who told her no."

He gave a little snort that might have been a laugh and climbed out of the cart with the hamburger buns.

"You are aware, I suppose, that Payton is a very pretty girl?" she asked as she accompanied him toward the porch. "You're in for a lot of this sort of thing in the future."

He nodded, his expression resigned. "She looks a lot like her mother."

So his late ex-wife had been a beauty. She couldn't help wondering what had gone wrong in the marriage, even though it was absolutely none of her business.

They entered the cabin together and Kix squeaked when she saw Maggie. "Are you going to have hamburgers with us, Maggie?" she asked, dashing to her side.

"Your dad invited me. I hope that's okay with everyone."

"You're very welcome, Maggie," Garrett's mother assured her with a warm smile from the kitchen counter, where she was slicing tomatoes.

"That grandmother of yours isn't coming, is she?"

Esther demanded. She sat in a chair facing the view of the lake, surrounded by books, a knitting bag and a teacup, her walker nearby. It looked as though she had claimed that spot permanently for her own.

"Mother," Paulette scolded, even as Garrett growled, "Meemaw."

"My grandmother isn't coming," Maggie replied lightly. "Just me."

"Good," Esther muttered.

Garrett sighed heavily in exasperation with his grandmother's rudeness, but didn't bother to argue any further with her, saying merely, "I'll start the grill."

"The patties are ready to go on as soon as the grill is hot enough," his mother informed him.

"Is there anything I can do to help?" Maggie asked.

Paulette shook her head. "Everything's almost ready. Why don't you chat with the girls? They always enjoy visiting with you."

"I love your top, Maggie." Payton studied the casual blouse closely. "That scoop neckline is very flattering."

"Thank you." Maggie had noticed that Payton was increasingly into fashion these days, always taking time to examine and comment on Maggie's outfits.

"Come upstairs and we'll show you where we sleep," Kix suggested eagerly. "We have a view of the lake from our window and it's really pretty."

"Maggie knows the cabin, Kix," Payton said with a shake of her head. "She owns it."

"My family owns it," Maggie corrected, "but it's been a while since I looked at the lake from that window." Actually, she'd inspected the cabin thoroughly hours before they'd settled in, but she saw no need to mention that. "Lead the way, Kix."

Kix dashed up the stairs and Maggie followed. Payton trailed them more slowly.

The loft had definitely been invaded by young girls, Maggie noted with a smile. Rather than the resort-furnished plain white sheets and coverlets, the two twin beds sported pink-and-green polka-dot sheets on one bed and yellow-and-green stripes on the other. From what she knew of their grandmother, she figured Paulette had been the one who'd insisted on bringing their own sheets rather than using the ones provided for guests. A shabby stuffed yellow bear sat on the polka-dot bed, which she figured must belong to Kix. Paperback books and teen magazines were strewn across the other bed. One of the drawers in the built-in dresser had been closed on the leg of a pair of ladybug-print pajamas.

"Look how pretty the shadows look on the lake now that the sun's getting lower," Kix said from the window.

Payton groaned. "Geez, Kix, she lives here. She sees the lake all the time."

"But I never get tired of it," Maggie replied, moving to admire the view. Dotted with boats and crisscrossed with rippling wakes, the lake glittered jewel-blue in the still bright, late-day sun.

Payton scowled. "Wish I could see the moon on the water with my new friends later. I met some really nice guys who are going down to the lake later to, you know, just throw rocks in the water and look at the stars and talk and stuff, and Dad acted like I asked if I could go to a bar or something."

"They got into another one of their fights," Kix confided. "Payton yells sometimes, but Daddy never does. He just says, 'That's final' in a really quiet voice. And you know from the way he says it that he's not going to change his mind no matter how much you beg or argue, but sometimes we do anyway, I guess, 'cause we hope maybe just once he'll listen. Like, Payton keeps asking for a red leather jacket like the one you wore last winter. She says she wants one like it for this next school year, but Dad keeps saying red leather isn't practical for school. And I want to stay up an hour later to watch TV because *all*—well, some—of my friends stay up until ten o'clock, but I have to go to bed at nine, which is a bedtime for babies. And I've asked him maybe a million times for a kitten, but all he'll say is 'we'll see.'"

"And you're his favorite." Payton tossed her head with a scowl. "He tells you yes a lot more than he does me." Payton whirled toward Maggie then. "I'm thirteen years old and he watches me like I'm a little kid. Like Kix."

"Hey!"

"All I wanted to do," Payton went on, ignoring her sister's indignant protest, "was to meet up with some friends. But just because they're boys, he said no. I mean, geez, what does he think is going to happen? He's here at the resort, their parents are here, a zillion other people are here, it's not like we're going to get into trouble. They're nice guys, Maggie. Trevor and Drake Ferguson. Do you know them?"

Maggie repeated what she'd said earlier to Garrett. "I've met them a few times when they've stayed here before. They seem like good kids."

"I know, right? Dad can be such a—"

"Payton!" Kix interrupted urgently, giving her sister a little shove.

For a moment it looked as though Payton might snarl at her sister, but her expression turned suddenly thoughtful. "Oh. Yeah, guess I shouldn't be talking about him that way. Family and all."

"Daddy's not really mean," Kix assured Maggie. "He's just overprotective. Grammy says that makes him a good father, but she's overprotective, too."

"I bet you'd have let me hang out with friends at the lake tonight if it were up to you, wouldn't you, Maggie?" Payton asked.

"Of course."

The teen nodded in satisfaction. "I knew it."

"As long as I was there, too," Maggie added. "I'd stay back out of the way. Maybe check email and stuff on my phone. But for someone your age out at night with a couple of teenage boys you just met, I'd say you need a discreet chaperone."

Payton rolled her eyes and fell backward on her bed. "Geez. I can't believe this."

Kix frowned at Maggie, who got the distinct feeling that she had just failed a test of some sort. But then the younger girl's expression cleared. "You're just trying to make Payton feel better about what Dad said, aren't you? So she won't be so mad at him."

"No, that's—"

"The burgers are ready," Paulette called from the foot of the stairs. "You girls ready to eat?"

Paulette seemed to consider Maggie one of the girls, even though she was fourteen years older than Payton. Maybe it was hearing Maggie grouped with her and Kix that made Payton forgive her for agreeing even in part with their dad. "Dad does make really good burgers," she conceded, climbing to her feet again.

Maggie smiled at her. "Then let's go get them while they're hot, shall we?"

* * *

After a leisurely dinner, Garrett walked Maggie out to the cart. "I'm glad you could join us. The whole family enjoyed having you."

She pulled her keys out of her pocket. "I had a nice time, too."

"The front-desk clerk told me when we checked in that it's going to be crazy busy around here this week."

Maggie chuckled. "For the rest of the summer, actually, but especially after Wednesday. A lot of people take a long weekend at the lake for the Fourth of July."

"I understand there's quite a celebration being planned here this weekend."

She nodded. "A fireworks show Thursday evening. A concert in the pavilion Friday evening. Carnival rides and inflatable bouncers in the pavilion area Saturday, with free cotton candy for the kids."

"That's a full schedule."

"Now that we've hired Rosie to take over reservations and check-ins, Hannah's had more time to develop marketing programs. She decided we should expand our traditional Independence Day celebrations. She's advertised it on social media and our webpage and with some flyers posted in local stores. We're charging a small admission fee for nonguests to help with the expenses and keep down the crowds a bit. We hope the effort will pay off in future business for the marina and the diner as well as the lodgings and campgrounds. I've been a little late getting to the holiday decorations, but I'll take care of that tomorrow."

"The weekend sounds like fun. I know the girls will get a kick out of it all."

"I hope so." She turned to him when they reached

the golf cart. "Thank you for inviting me for dinner, Garrett. I enjoyed it very much."

"Payton seems to be in a much better mood now."

Was that really the only reason he'd wanted her to have dinner with them? To entertain his daughters? But then again, why else? She reminded herself that she wasn't looking to get personally involved with this over-taxed single dad, anyway.

"Well, good night," she said, putting a hand on top of the cart in preparation for climbing behind the wheel. "I'll see you tomorrow at the birthday party, if not before."

She thought his gaze focused momentarily on her lips. Had they been parting after another type of out-ing—say, the type of date she would never have with him—the evening might well have ended with a kiss. She found her thoughts wandering into forbidden terri-tory as she looked at his firm mouth and imagined how it would feel covering her own. Abruptly clearing her throat, she almost leaped into the golf cart.

"Good night, Garrett," she blurted again.

She barely gave him a chance to reply before she was buzzing away.

Maggie was so busy Tuesday she didn't have a chance to eat lunch until after two that afternoon. In addition to her usual responsibilities supervising the cleaning staff, the extra holiday-week business added quite a bit of work. She was training two new employ-ees that week. One was an older, experienced maid; the other, a young woman named Darby Burns, had never worked in housekeeping but seemed very eager to learn.

Later, Maggie spent a couple hours inventorying and ordering supplies. She'd even hung some bunting at the motel. There was no lobby for the sixteen-unit lakeside inn—all the rooms opened to the outside, with a covered breezeway separating the two wings—so she had draped bunting on the concrete walls, adding a cheery pop of red, white and blue for guests on their way to their rooms or the ice maker and vending machines in the breezeway.

Finally taking a break, she left the motel and walked briskly to the main administrative building. Pushing through the double doors, she stepped into the big foyer, her nose twitching in response to the delicious scents of grilled sandwiches and simmering soup-of-the-day wafting from the diner.

The box of decorations and a stepladder still waited for her in the corner behind the desk, but she would resume decorating after she ate. In addition to what she and her staff had done at the motel that morning, her dad and Aaron and their small crew had been working outside, preparing the grounds for the fireworks show, concert and carnival. Her dad would fret all week about any potential damage to his immaculate landscaping.

She turned right to enter the diner. Few people were eating lunch this late in the afternoon, though three older couples probably staying in the RV grounds were chatting over soup at a large back-corner table. Two tanned, middle-aged men in Western boots and hats and faded denim sat at one end of the bar drinking coffee, probably just in from fishing.

Sarah Bell smiled from behind the counter when Maggie entered. "What can I get for you, hon?"

Sliding onto a bar stool at the other end of the counter from the fishing cowboys, Maggie replied, "I'm starving. I'll take whatever is fast."

"Chicken corn chowder today."

"Perfect."

Moments later, her aunt set a steaming bowl of soup and a square of jalapeño corn bread in front of her. Maggie dug in gratefully. She had eaten about half of her meal when she heard her name squealed from the doorway in a familiar soprano.

"It's Maggie. Hi, Maggie!"

Swiveling on her stool, Maggie saw Garrett's entire family entering the diner. Kix was followed by her sister, grandmother and great-grandmother. Garrett brought up the rear.

Wearing denim shorts and a pink T-shirt with pink flip-flops, her bright red hair barely confined to loosening braids, Kix dashed to Maggie's side. "We went swimming this morning and then we had lunch and then we went for a ride in the boat and it was fun and then I said I wanted to come to the diner and Daddy said okay but I can't have a milk shake because we're having cake and ice cream at my party tonight and that's too much ice cream in one day. But he said I can have a soda and maybe I can get a milk shake some other day while we're here."

Maggie was accustomed enough by now to Kix's breathless, stream-of-consciousness style of conversation to follow along fairly easily. She reached out to give the girl a hug. "Happy birthday, Kix."

Kix nearly strangled her with her enthusiastic return embrace. "Thanks, Maggie. It's been the best birthday ever! I'm eleven now. Almost a teenager!"

Garrett gave a heartfelt groan.

"I'm sure my aunt Sarah can arrange for you to have a soda. I recommend the cherry Italian soda. It's my favorite," Maggie said with a smile, gently disentangling herself from Kix's arms.

Sarah agreed cheerily. "Have a seat and I'll fix you right up."

Garrett and the girls had been into the diner during summer swimming and boating visits, but this was the first time the older members of his family had joined them at the resort. Maggie wasn't sure how much that had to do with the long-standing rivalry between her grandmother and Garrett's.

On Maggie's recommendation, everyone requested cherry sodas except Garrett, who ordered coffee. They settled at a table near the bar, pulling up an extra chair so Kix and Payton could crowd together on one side. Sarah served glasses of fizzy pink soda topped with dollops of fresh whipped cream and cherries. Garrett chuckled when she slipped him a cherry to accompany his plain black coffee. He bit the candied fruit off the stem, then set the stem aside.

Maggie turned sideways so she could visit with the family while she finished her lunch. She didn't actually have to stop eating to talk. Hyper with excitement about her special day, Kix rattled on almost without stopping to take sips of her soda. Her upper lip dotted with whipped cream, she told Maggie about the special breakfast they'd had—her favorite cinnamon-apple French toast—and about the wildlife they'd seen during their cruise around the lake. Payton managed to break in a few times to talk, and the older women chatted a bit with Sarah.

Maggie listened to it all, keenly aware of Garrett quietly sipping his coffee while his family talked. It seemed that every time she glanced at him he was looking back at her. Probably just coincidence, but each time she looked away quickly, making an effort to appear casual about it. She was entirely too drawn to him, especially considering he was sitting there with his daughters, two of the primary reasons that nothing was likely to come from her attraction to him. She and Garrett were unlikely ever to be more than casual friends. Which didn't mean she couldn't fantasize a little....

"Are you working this afternoon?" Kix asked her a bit too casually. "Daddy said we can't bother you if you're working, but if you aren't, maybe you want to play games with us or something? We brought our tennis rackets and a basketball and a volleyball and some board games for if it rains but it's really nice today and not rainy at all, so..."

"Kix," Garrett murmured.

"I know." She sighed heavily. "Breathe."

"Right."

Maggie couldn't help laughing. "I would love to play with you, Kix, and I promise I'll try sometime while you're here, but this afternoon I'm helping decorate the lobby for the festivities this weekend. We're starting in just a few minutes. I'll be there this evening for your birthday cake, though."

Though she'd initially looked disappointed, Kix's face lit up. "I love to decorate. Can I help? And Payton, too?"

"Kix," her dad said quickly, "you'd be in the way. Why don't we shoot some hoops instead?"

"I wouldn't get in the way," Kix argued, looking at Maggie with hopeful eyes. "I'd do everything Maggie said and I'd help a lot."

"They're both welcome to help decorate if that's how Kix wants to spend part of her birthday," Maggie assured Garrett. "I'll keep a close eye on them if you want to let them stay for a while."

Kix bounced in excitement. Payton even forgot to look bored. "I like decorating, too," she said.

Garrett's mother frowned. "I thought we were all going to spend time together this week."

Maggie wondered immediately if she'd made a mistake inviting the girls to help her decorate. Their grandmother looked so disapproving that she couldn't help asking herself if she'd made a gaffe.

Garrett must have sensed her discomfort. He gave her a slight shake of his head, then addressed his mother. "You and Meemaw both said you'd like to take a nap this afternoon before the birthday party. You weren't expecting the girls to watch you sleep, were you?"

His mother cleared her throat. "Well, no, but I thought you would be doing something with the girls."

He turned to Kix. "You can help for a little while, if Maggie is sure you won't be in the way, but I expect you to follow her instructions to the letter. I'm leaving my cell number with her and I want her to call me if there are any problems. I'll be back to collect you in time for you to wash up and have dinner before the birthday party."

"Don't go wandering off," their grandmother added, still looking anxious. "Stay in the building with Miss Maggie. And don't be climbing any ladders or handling anything electrical. And—"

"Give it a rest, Paulette," Esther ordered. "They'll be fine."

Garrett drained the last of his coffee and stood. "Come on, let's get you two down for your naps. And I'm not talking to the kids."

Maggie bit her lip to prevent a grin, which probably would not be appreciated by his mother. Garrett paid for the beverages, gave Maggie his phone number, reminded his daughters one last time to be good, then ushered the older women toward the door.

They had almost made it out when Maggie's cousin Shelby and their grandmother entered. Maggie fancied that she could almost feel the tension settle into the room. The two cowboys at the other end of the bar glanced around as if sensing an impending shootout.

Telling herself not to be silly, she shook her head and stood with a bright smile. "Mimi, you remember the McHale family, don't you? Today is Kix's eleventh birthday. She and her sister, Payton, are going to help us decorate for a while."

She congratulated herself on thinking to casually mention Kix's birthday. Surely the older women could set their differences aside to avoid any unpleasantness on such a happy occasion. Mimi had always been gracious enough to Garrett and the girls on the few times they'd crossed paths, despite their connection to her enemy.

Her ploy worked. Both Mimi and Esther immediately forced their stern mouths into somewhat softer lines.

"Hello, Esther," Mimi said coolly.

"Dixie," Esther replied with a curt nod, her tone just as frosty.

"Happy birthday, Kix," perky blonde Shelby said, characteristic warmth in her smiling blue eyes when she turned to the youngest McHale. "We're going to have fun decorating. I'm glad you're joining us."

Grinning ear to ear, Kix expressed her eagerness to get started. Paulette was still fussing at the girls to be careful when Garrett finally ushered her out.

Mimi shook her head as she watched the trio leave. "That grandmother of yours is a worrywart, isn't she, girls?"

"Mimi," Maggie murmured in warning, dragging her attention back to the room. Maybe she'd gotten a bit distracted watching Garrett leave, but now she had to make sure her own tactless grandmother didn't say anything to distress the girls.

"She's right, Maggie," Payton said with a heavy sigh. "Grammy worries about *everything*. She drives us crazy."

"Crazy," Kix echoed with a fervent nod.

"That just means she loves you very much," Sarah said briskly, silently daring her mother-in-law to continue that particular conversation. "Kix, maybe you'd like to help me put up some decorations here in the dining room? I have some flag decals for the windows and some little flags in vases for the tables and some bunting to hang behind the counter. I can work with you now since there are no customers at the moment."

Kix looked thrilled to work in the diner. Knowing her aunt would enjoy working with the girl, Maggie led Payton into the foyer to get started in there. She tucked Garrett's phone number into her pocket before opening the first box.

Chapter Three

With his mother and grandmother napping and his daughters busy decorating, Garrett took advantage of the time alone and the nice weather for a brisk walk around the resort. It was a sunny afternoon but a nice breeze kept it from feeling too hot, and he enjoyed the outing. Usually he ran several miles a day, a way of staying in shape and working out some of his frustrations, but today he settled for walking at a fast clip around the perimeter of the resort, probably a couple miles in total.

Leaving the cabin, he veered right, in the opposite direction from the marina. After entering through the front gate, the main road formed a big rectangle within the resort. It passed the pavilion and playground, then the motel and the first three of the eight detached cabins before leading to the main building housing the diner, store, offices and marina. Next, one would drive past the boat launch and day-use picnic and swimming area, the row of cabins that included the one in which Garrett's family was staying, and then into the campgrounds. RV pads with water and electricity lay along the lakeside and lined the two smaller roads that bisected the resort. Wooded tent-camping grounds were located in the center of the compound, still within view of the glittering water.

Even on this weekday the lake was filled with boaters, skiers, personal watercraft and swimmers. He spotted one distant sailboat, its sails white against the blue sky. The campgrounds weren't yet full, but he passed quite a few elaborate RVs with hydraulic extensions and awnings and smaller vehicles that had been pulled behind with tow bars. Some had maybe stopped for a night or two on their way to the Gulf coast, he figured, noting license tags from Oklahoma, Nebraska and Arkansas. Others were perhaps regulars who came to fish and visit with camping friends and otherwise escape the daily grind.

A young couple on bicycles, the man with a toddler in a seat on the back of his bike, passed in the other direction, exchanging waves and casual greetings with Garrett. A large, barrel-chested man walking a Chihuahua on a sparkly leash tipped his ten-gallon hat when he and Garrett crossed paths. "How's it going?"

"Good, thanks," Garrett answered. "You?"

"Ridin' high, thankee. Here for some fishing?"

Having been raised in Texas, Garrett was accustomed to garrulous strangers striking up conversation. "Here with my kids for the week."

"Well, ain't that nice. You have a good 'un."

"Same to you."

"Let's go, Prissy," the big man said to his wandering little dog, giving a slight tug on the leash.

Smiling, Garrett continued on his way.

Looping around the end of the resort, he started up the other side toward the marina. The tent grounds were on his left now, woods on his right. On the other side of those trees, accessed by a private drive, were the homes of the Bell family. He'd never been into the private compound, but Maggie had once mentioned that three houses and four manufactured homes housed the various family members who worked in the resort. One of the mobile homes belonged to Hannah, who used it when she and her husband and baby were here. The others belonged to Maggie and Shelby and Steven, who'd held on to his place here even though he was pursuing career goals elsewhere.

Not for the first time, he wondered what it had been like for Maggie growing up here, and whether she had any professional goals beyond working for the resort for the rest of her life. Not that he considered that an unworthy ambition in itself. He was simply curious about her. Very curious.

Just as he reached the Private Drive sign, a heavy-duty green utility cart paused at the end of the drive. He nodded when he recognized Aaron Walker in the driver's seat. He'd met Aaron a couple of times and he seemed like a decent guy.

Dark-haired, dark-eyed Aaron leaned out of the cart to shake Garrett's hand. "Nice to see you," he said. "Enjoying your stay?"

"Very much, thanks. We took the boat out for a while earlier. The girls saw a couple of herons and egrets and a raccoon at the edge of the water. Kix especially loves seeing wildlife."

"Go out early and you're likely to see some deer in the coves."

"I'll take her out tomorrow morning. Maybe fish a little."

They dawdled a few more minutes, talking about the most likely nearby spots for Kix to catch a fish, then Aaron had to move on. He and Bryan were stringing red, white and blue lights on the pavilion this afternoon, he explained. The back of the cart was filled with supplies he'd brought from storage. "You need a lift?"

Garrett shook his head. "Thanks, but I'm enjoying the walk."

Aaron pulled his green resort cap down on his forehead. "See you around."

Garrett waited until the cart buzzed away before walking on. He figured he might as well go straight to the main building and get the girls. It had been almost two hours since he'd left them, and Maggie was probably ready to get them out of her hair.

He knew his girls would get a kick out of the upcoming festivities. They'd been in surprisingly cheerful moods so far today, despite Payton's inability to resist the occasional dig at his excessive rules—in her opinion. Maybe Kix's idea of a family retreat, while unexpected, had been a good one after all. He had to admit there had been too much tension in his house lately as the girls had rebelled in their own ways against his stricter expectations than they'd had with their mother. The methods he'd used as an air force major to supervise young airmen didn't seem to work nearly as well with a couple of adolescent daughters.

Stepping through the entry door, he saw that the lobby was already transformed from when he'd left. Flags and bunting festooned nearly every surface. Payton and Kix, assisted by Shelby, seemed to be looking for places to add even more. Maggie's mom stood in the doorway of the store, watching the activities with a smile while keeping an eye on the few customers browsing among her shelves. Patriotic decals clung to the glass walls of the diner and store. Through the decorated glass he could see that business was picking up as the early dinner crowd shuffled in.

He didn't see Maggie at first. And then he spotted her behind the counter, precariously balanced on a stepladder as she stretched up to place one last bunting rosette high on the wall. Shaking his head, he moved to steady the ladder, wondering why no one else had thought to do so. She smiled down at him. "Your cheeks are flushed."

"I've been walking. The wind is picking up a bit."

He stood eye level with her breasts, something he was trying hard to ignore. Being the healthy male that he was, he wasn't doing a particularly good job of it. They were so nicely outlined by her purple wrap top. He kept his eyes focused upward on her face instead—which wasn't exactly a hardship. "You've gotten a lot done since I left."

She straightened the rosette in the bare space she'd been trying to fill. "We've had some good helpers. The girls worked very hard."

That didn't surprise him. Once his daughters became enthused about something, they gave it their all. Maggie started down the ladder and he put a hand on the small of her back to steady her. It was an automatic gesture he made without thinking. Yet when he felt the warmth of her through her clothing, felt the curve of her spine beneath his hand, felt the ripple of muscle when she climbed down, his entire body reacted with a surge of awareness that caught him off guard. He dropped his hand almost too abruptly, stepping back quickly out of her way.

"Too bad we don't hang mistletoe for Independence Day," Kix said, wide-eyed and innocent as she gazed at them. "It's fun hanging mistletoe at Christmastime, right?"

Garrett raised an eyebrow. Surely his daughter wasn't suggesting he should kiss Maggie?

Maggie chuckled. "I don't think we want to deal with mistletoe year-round, Kix. My grandfather would try to hang out here in the lobby and kiss all the pretty girls who come in."

Shelby laughed musically. "You've got that right. Pop docs like to flirt."

Payton and Kix stood in the center of the lobby to look around critically. "Does it look good, Maggie?" Payton asked. "Miss Linda, do you see any empty places?"

Maggie and her mother made a show of studying the room from every angle, tilting their heads and narrowing their eyes. Both declared it to be perfect, an opinion solemnly endorsed by Shelby and Rosie.

"This must be the most patriotic resort lobby in all of Texas," Maggie added, reaching for the two big boxes that had held decorations.

"Let me help you with those," Garrett offered.

Maggie smiled at him over the armload. "I'm just taking them upstairs to the storage room."

He relieved her of the stack without giving her a chance to protest. Shrugging, she turned and led the way upstairs.

It was the first time Garrett had been upstairs in the big building. He noted the tidy office spaces, the well-organized storage rooms filled with supplies and seasonal decorations and the sweeping view of the marina and the lake from big back windows. There was very little clutter and no dust that he could see; he'd bet Maggie was the one responsible for that. Cabin six had been immaculate when he and his family had settled in, and he'd once overheard two Sunday-morning resort guests agree that the motel was one of the cleanest lodgings they'd ever patronized. He suspected she supervised her staff closely but fairly. He already knew she didn't shy away from hard work herself—just one more thing he found to admire about Maggie Bell.

His daughters were still admiring their handiwork when he and Maggie rejoined them downstairs a few minutes later. "Isn't it beautiful, Daddy?" Kix breathed, spinning in a circle in the gaily bedecked lobby.

He smoothed the flyaway red hair she'd inherited from her mother's family. "Yes, it is. Great job."

"We had fun."

"I'm sure you did. Maybe you should thank Maggie for letting you help."

"We're the ones in their debt," Linda replied with a smile, coming out of the store. "They worked very hard. And to show our appreciation..."

She handed each of the girls a reusable green market bag emblazoned with the resort's bell-shaped logo. "Here's a souvenir water bottle for each of you. And Kix, because it's your birthday I added a little something extra for you."

Kix squealed in pleasure when she drew a little stuffed toy from the bag. The smiling, six-inch stuffed raccoon wore a green resort-logo T-shirt. Garrett felt a moment of gratitude that his little girl was still young enough to appreciate a toy. His daughters were growing up much too fast.

"I love him," Kix said, hugging the raccoon. "I'm going to name him Belly after the resort. Thank you, Miss Linda."

Maggie's mom hugged Kix, wished her happy birthday again, then moved back into the store to relieve her mother-in-law at the register.

"That was very generous of her," Garrett murmured to Maggie.

Maggie smiled. "Mom loves kids. She's already started spoiling my niece terribly."

He glanced at his watch. "We'd better head back to the cabin, girls. We have things to do there before the party."

This would be Kix's second birthday party. He and his mother had hosted a group of her friends at a local pizza parlor Saturday afternoon. His head had hurt for an hour after that giggle-fest. It hadn't helped that one of Kix's friends had a single mom who'd stayed for the party and determinedly hit on him at every opportunity. He hadn't let it go to his ego; she'd flirted just as enthusiastically with the good-looking waiter. Garrett thought she'd have left the restaurant with whichever one responded first to her overtures, her daughter's presence notwithstanding. While he would never punish a child for her mother's behavior, he had made a mental note never to let Kix visit that particular friend at the girl's home. They could meet at his or his mother's house instead.

No one would be flirting with him at tonight's party. Not that he'd mind so much this time, he thought, watching Maggie as she thanked the girls for their help and assured them she would see them later for cake. A guy could fantasize, right?

* * *

Maggie thought about walking from her mobile home to the cabin for the birthday party, but she was a little tired from her busy day. She decided to take a golf cart again instead. There were always carts around for the family's use.

She'd showered and changed out of her work clothes for the party, dressing in slim jeans, heeled sandals and a drape-neck sleeveless red top. She wore her favorite earrings, tricolored metal dangles that her sister had given her. Climbing into the cart, she set her gift for the party on the seat beside her. She hoped Kix would like it.

It was just before seven when she stopped in front of cabin six. She was a bit surprised to see a couple of extra cars in the driveway. Having heard about the prior party, she'd thought this one was just for the family. She carried the brightly wrapped gift to the door, which opened before she had a chance to knock. Kix must have been watching for her. "Hi, Maggie! Come in."

She couldn't help laughing in response to the enthusiastic greeting—as if they hadn't just parted a couple hours earlier. "Hi, Kix. Happy birthday yet again."

Kix giggled. "Thank you yet again."

Tugged inside by the girl, Maggie noted that a few balloons and streamers had been scattered around the main room and a cake with pink frosting and eleven as-yet unlit candles sat in the center of the bar. Esther sat in the armchair with the view of the lake while Paulette bustled around in the kitchen, chatting with another woman of about her own age. She spotted Garrett through the glass doors, standing outside on the deck talking to two other men. The lowering sun cast intriguing shadows across his face, and her heart fluttered in instinctive reaction.

His eyes met hers through the glass and she saw him say something to his companions before reaching to open the door. The three men entered just as Paulette noticed Maggie's presence. She hurried to greet her.

"Kix, why didn't you tell us Maggie's here? Come on in, Maggie, and meet our guests. You know Reverend Bettencourt, of course. And this is my husband's sister, Coralee, and her husband, Mickey Lovett. They're here this evening to celebrate Kix's birthday with us."

Maggie shook hands with the older couple, then exchanged warm greetings with Jay, all the while aware of Garrett standing nearby watching her.

Paulette wanted to get the party started immediately. She snapped photos with a little digital camera when Garrett lit the candles and everyone gathered around the cake to sing the "Happy Birthday" song. Kix blew out the tiny flames with a big gust of breath, earning a round of applause. She responded with a giggle and a bow. "May I open my presents before we eat the cake?" she asked eagerly, waving toward a small, colorful pile of packages.

Given permission, she ripped into the stack. She shrieked in delight at each of her gifts. Her great-grandmother had crocheted a floppy pink-and-white beach hat in loose, airy stitches dotted with lime-green plastic beads. It was so cute Maggie immediately wanted one herself. Kix obviously loved it every bit as much as the department store gift card that accompanied it. A hot pink digital camera from her grandmother made Kix start to bounce again and announce her plans to take "a million" pictures of the lake tomorrow.

Her great-aunt and uncle had brought her a pretty

silver-bead bracelet from which dangled a silver heart engraved with the letter *K,* which earned them each a hug. Payton gave her a couple of favorite films on Blu-ray for their home library, both of which seemed to please her greatly. "We'll watch them together," Kix promised her sister.

Jay had purchased another gift card, this one for ebooks. "Your dad said you like buying books for your ebook reader."

Kix beamed. "Yes, I do, Uncle Jay. I love to read. Thank you."

"You're welcome, sweetheart."

The last gift in the stack was the one from Maggie. Like Esther's, hers was handmade—a denim shoulder bag lined with a bright pink floral fabric and fastened with a big pink plastic button. On the front of the bag was an appliquéd white sleeping kitten wearing a pink ribbon bow. Beneath the kitten, Maggie had machine-embroidered Kix's name in flowing hot pink script.

Judging by her shrill squeak, Kix was a bit more than satisfied with the gift. "A purse! And it has a kitten. And my name! Maggie, it's so pretty. Thank you."

She patted the girl's back when she received an enthusiastic hug. "You're welcome, sweetie. I hope you'll enjoy it."

"I love it! I'll carry it every day."

"Did you make this, Maggie?" Esther asked, closely examining the bag. "Very nice work."

"Yes, I did, and thank you. My grandmother taught me to sew when I was young, but I've started learning appliqué and embroidery since my niece was born last year. I've made her a few monogrammed things. Shelby and her mom like to quilt, so they've made all the nursery beddings. Little Claire is already in danger of being quite spoiled," she added with a laugh.

"Your grandmother was always an adequate seam-stress," Esther conceded rather royally. "I believe she finished as high as second to me a few times in our home economics sewing competitions."

Maggie had to make a massive effort not to laugh in response to Esther's smugness over those high school victories sixty-plus years ago. Just showed that people didn't really change that much on the inside, even as the passing years took their toll on the outside, she mused.

Kix was already stashing her gift cards in her new bag. "Look, Daddy. Isn't it pretty? Maggie always knows how to dress just right, doesn't she?"

"Yes, she does," Garrett agreed easily. "Doesn't mean either of you girls is getting a red leather coat for this coming winter just because Maggie has one," he added with a meaningful look toward Payton.

Payton released an exasperated sigh. "It wouldn't have to be *real* leather," she grumbled.

"Garrett, aren't you going to give Kix your gift?" Paulette prodded.

Garrett plucked a small wrapped box from the top of the fridge and handed it to his younger daughter. "You changed my plans a bit when you asked to spend the week here," he said to Kix. "Open it and I'll explain."

Looking curiously puzzled, Kix pulled away the wrapping paper and lifted the lid of the square white box inside. "It's a bracelet," she said, drawing out a narrow pink leather circle fastened with a silver buckle and studded with a few tiny rhinestones. She shook it lightly and a little silver bell tinkled. "It's cute, Daddy."

Payton groaned dramatically. "Wow, Kix, sometimes you can be so dense."

Jay chuckled. "I don't think that's a bracelet, Kix."

Kix caught her breath. "A collar? A kitty collar? Really, Daddy, I can have a kitten?"

Smiling wryly, he nodded. "I'll take you to the shelter to choose one next week. I'd have taken you today, but it will be better to wait until we're back home."

She launched herself at him. "Thank you, thank you, thank you!"

Loosening her stranglehold around his neck enough to allow him to speak, he said, "You're welcome. But don't think I'm going to be cleaning the litter box or putting out food and water. That's all on you. Like I've been telling you, owning a living creature is a major responsibility. The first sign I see that the cat isn't receiving proper care, we'll be looking for a new home for it."

Kix bobbed her head in eager agreement. "I'll clean the litter box every day. And I'll feed it and water it and brush it and play with it and teach it tricks and love it soooo much."

"Good luck with that teaching-a-cat-tricks part, huh?" Jay murmured to Maggie.

Both touched and amused by the child's joy, Maggie smiled at Jay. "Seriously. But I like cats, too. I've thought of getting one for myself."

"I already have one," he confessed. "A big, battered old tom I call Frankie, short for Frankenstein. He adopted me right after I moved back here and the two of us get along very well together. Kix is crazy about him, and he tolerates her when she visits."

She chuckled, enjoying the mental image he'd created. She wouldn't have pegged Jay as a cat guy. But then, she didn't know that much about his personal life, really. As generous as he was with his time and compassion for the community, she sensed there were parts of himself he kept quite private. She suspected he was a man who had known pain and heartache firsthand. Perhaps those personal trials had made it easier for him to connect with his congregation, especially in their times of distress.

She glanced around toward the others and her gaze clashed with Garrett's. He was frowning a bit when she met his eyes, but his expression quickly smoothed back into a polite smile. "I've probably lost my mind," he said.

She laughed. "I bet Kix will take good care of her kitten. She's certainly old enough to handle the responsibility."

"I know, right?" Kix beamed up at Maggie. "I knew you would understand."

"Who's ready for cake and ice cream?" Paulette asked, setting aside the camera she'd been using to snap photos of Kix opening her gifts.

"I am!" Kix said to no one's surprise.

Telling herself she must have imagined some hidden meaning in the expression she'd seen on Garrett's face, Maggie joined the others in line for birthday cake.

Kix's grandmother and great-aunt efficiently distributed slices of strawberry cake topped with scoops of vanilla ice cream. While the five senior members of the party gathered around the table, Garrett joined his girls, Maggie and Jay in the living room. Kix and Payton sat cross-legged on the floor, using the coffee table for a dining table, while Maggie sat on the couch and Garrett and Jay in chairs nearby. Garrett had suggested moving the party out to the deck where they could enjoy the pleasant evening weather, but he'd been overruled by his grandmother and aunt, both of whom preferred to remain indoors.

There was little chance for the adults to talk during the desserts with both girls chattering, but everyone seemed to enjoy the girls' enthusiasm. Garrett didn't even bother to remind Kix to breathe during her jumbled monologues, indulging her on her birthday.

Somehow the conversation wound around to Garrett's career. "Sometimes Dad lets me take the controls," Payton boasted, far from the first time she'd mentioned her love of flying to Maggie. "I'm going to get my private pilot's license when I'm fifteen, right, Dad?"

He gave a little shrug toward Maggie. "Payton's obsessed with flying. I guess she got that from me."

"I want to be an airline pilot," Payton informed everyone firmly, though Garrett doubted there was anyone in the room who hadn't already heard that aspiration. "Dad said the best way to do that is to get military training, so I'll probably go to the air force academy like he did."

Paulette was not at all happy with that plan and she never missed a chance to point it out. "There's plenty of time for you to decide what you want to do, Payton. I still think you should consider medical school. You're so good in your science classes and you'd be a wonderful doctor."

Having heard that suggestion many times before, Payton merely shrugged and took another bite of her cake. Garrett might have described her expression as mulishly stubborn. He'd told his mom before that the most surefire way to get Payton to do something was to try to discourage her from doing it, but his mom still felt compelled to argue every time her granddaughter mentioned the military. He had mixed feelings about the idea himself—partially because he wasn't ready to think about Payton growing up and leaving home—but he'd always said he would support his girls in their career goals.

"I want to be a veterinarian," Kix announced. "I want to take care of sick cats. Dogs, too, but cats are my favorite."

"Do you like to fly, Maggie?" Payton asked, proving her thoughts were still focused on her own envisioned future.

"I haven't flown much," Maggie admitted. "Just a few times on commercial airlines. It's sort of a hassle these days, but I don't really mind it too badly."

Payton looked surprised. "You've never been up in a small plane?"

"No, I haven't had the chance. Maybe I will someday."

"You should take her up, Daddy," Kix urged quickly. "It's fun, Maggie. Daddy's a good pilot, so you wouldn't have to be scared."

Garrett was caught by surprise at the sudden suggestion.

"I'm sure he is," Maggie said lightly, her expression hard to read. "But—"

"You could take her up tomorrow, Dad," Payton chimed in. "We don't have any other plans for tomorrow, and Kix and I are going to help Grammy make cookies, aren't we, Grammy? We have new cookie cutters shaped like tropical fish and sea horses, and Grammy brought food coloring and sprinkles and stuff to decorate them with."

"I did promise to let you help with baking," their grandmother agreed, her eyes lighting with anticipation of sharing that activity with her granddaughters. "Of course, there's not quite as much room in this kitchen as there would have been at home, but we can spread out on the table."

"So you can take Maggie flying while we're cooking with Grammy," Kix told her father in satisfaction.

"Take her up in the Cessna one-fifty," Payton instructed. "You'll love that one, Maggie. It's a cute little two-seater and it's a high-wing so you can see great."

"Oh, well, I—"

"Maggie probably has to work tomorrow," Garrett said with a repressive frown at his daughters. "It's still a weekday, and it's a holiday week, so you've seen how busy the resort is."

"Maybe she could take off a little early tomorrow afternoon," Jay murmured with a grin, apparently enjoying the interplay.

Garrett gave him a look, then glanced at Maggie. "I'd be happy to take you up anytime you'd like, but don't let these yahoos pressure you into it."

Kix giggled at being called a yahoo. Jay chuckled. Payton, of course, rolled her eyes.

"Well, actually, I could probably take off an hour early tomorrow afternoon," she said. "If I start a bit earlier than usual, I could be done by four, maybe."

The words must have escaped her impulsively; almost as soon as she'd said them, she looked rather surprised to hear them. Or maybe he was projecting his own surprise onto her.

"Oh. So, um, want to go up for an aerial sightseeing tour of the lake?" he offered, feeling all eyes focused on him. "I can show you how the resort looks from fifteen hundred feet up."

"That does sound like fun," she admitted.

Maybe a little too much fun, he thought with a swallow. "You know, I can get a four-seater if you girls want to go up with us," he said.

Kix started to say something, but he'd have sworn her sister poked her under the coffee table. "We go up all the time," Payton said then with a casual wave of her hand. "We promised Grammy we'd help her make cookies. She's going to teach me how to make the dough from scratch."

"Me, too," Kix echoed. "From scratch."

"So you and Maggie go ahead," Payton continued. "Tomorrow's like a holiday. Both of you usually have to work weekday afternoons, so you might as well take advantage of having a little time off, right?"

Maggie's laugh sounded a little self-conscious. "I'm not sure it's time off for your dad to take up a sight-seer. That's pretty much another day at work for him, isn't it?"

"Not if he's doing it because he wants to and it's not for pay," Kix assured her. "Daddy likes to fly, don't you, Daddy?"

"Yes," he said. "I do. Um, Jay, want to come along?"

"I'd love to," his friend answered promptly. "But I've got appointments tomorrow afternoon and a rehearsal dinner to attend tomorrow evening for a couple I'm marrying Thursday evening."

"Thursday evening?" Coralee echoed. "That's an unusual night for a wedding."

Jay nodded. "Nice young couple on a tight budget and schedule. They're having rehearsal tomorrow, a very small wedding ceremony Thursday, then taking a three-day weekend for a quick honeymoon in Galveston before Art has to return to his job on Monday."

"A no-fuss affair," Mickey said. "Best kind."

"Honeymoons don't mean as much these days," Garrett's grandmother commented dryly. "Most young couples have dinner before saying grace, if you know what I mean."

Kix looked a little confused by the adage, but Jay quickly changed the subject. "This strawberry cake was delicious, Paulette. One of the best I ever had."

Garrett's mother beamed in pleasure, offering him another slice. Jay declined politely.

"Let's play Uno," Kix suggested, springing to her feet. "Maggie, Uncle Jay, you want to play a game with us?"

"Well, I—"

"I really should be—"

Kix interrupted them with her patented big-eyed look. "It would be a birthday party game. For my birthday."

Garrett groaned. "Kix—"

"I could probably stay for one game of Uno," Maggie assured Kix with a quick smile.

Jay proved equally susceptible to a little girl's blatant manipulation. "Sure, why not. One game."

Kix was able to talk everyone but her great-grandmother into playing. Esther sat in the chair she'd claimed as her own and watched, occasionally cheating by warning the others about the cards she could see in Garrett's hand. He didn't really care if he won, but he started hiding his cards from her anyway, just on principle.

After the promised game—which Payton won, to her smug satisfaction—Jay and Maggie both insisted they had to leave, as did Garrett's aunt and uncle. Amid the hugs and good-nights, Maggie drew out her keys.

"You want to meet at four tomorrow for our flight?" Garrett asked her at the door.

She glanced toward the girls, who were bidding good-night to Jay. "You're sure they didn't persuade you to do something you'd rather not do?"

"No, it's always fun to take up a small-plane newbie. You'll find that it's quite a bit different from flying commercial."

"I've always wanted to go up in a small plane," she confessed. "Just never got around to it. I'm looking forward to it."

"So am I." *A bit too much for comfort, actually.* "So I'll meet you in front of the main building at four?"

"I'll be there."

Jay joined them at the door. "I'll be honored to escort you to your car, Ms. Bell," he offered Maggie teasingly.

"It's a golf cart, but I'll still accept the escort," she replied, her tone equally light. "Good night, Garrett."

"Good night." He watched as Jay gallantly held out an arm to assist Maggie down the front steps. She accepted with a laugh. Garrett closed the door with a sharp click, unreasonably irked at the sight of Jay and Maggie laughing together.

"Taking Maggie flying will be fun, won't it, Daddy?" Kix asked, just a little too artlessly.

Suspicious, he looked from one of his daughters to the other, his eyes narrowed on their too-innocent expressions. Speaking in a low voice so as not to be overheard by his mother in the kitchen or his grandmother, who'd already gone back to her room to get ready for bed, he asked, "You girls aren't up to anything, are you? Like trying to match up me and Maggie? Because if you are—"

"You and Maggie?" Payton snorted dramatically. "Yeah, right, Dad."

"Yeah, right," Kix parroted.

"Actually," Payton added, "we were thinking Maggie and Uncle Jay make kind of a cute couple. Don't you think?"

"No, I don't think." He'd answered a bit curtly; he couldn't quite explain even to himself why the very suggestion was so disturbing to him.

"Why not?" Payton demanded, as if sensing his thought.

Because Jay was only a year younger than he was, he could have retorted, which also made him too old for Maggie. And because Jay's relationship status was complicated, to say the least, though Garrett wasn't at liberty to discuss what he knew of his friend's personal life. And because…well, just because. But all he said was, "You girls don't need to be playing matchmaker with anyone. Just mind your own business, okay?"

Payton shrugged. "Whatever."

A shrug was her second favorite nonanswer, right after an eye roll. He sighed. "Kix, go start your bath. I'm going to check email."

"Okay, Daddy. Thank you again for the kitten I'm going to get. I hope the shelter has a white kitten. Or maybe a gray one. Or a calico. Calicoes are pretty, too. What do you think, Payton? I've already picked out a name. Misty. Or maybe Breezy. Or Ariel. What name do you like? Maybe—"

"Kix," Garrett said wearily, reaching up to rub his forehead.

She sighed. "I know. Bath."

Satisfied that she was following through on his instructions, Garrett headed for his room to check his email. Not that he was expecting any important messages. He simply needed a few moments of peace and quiet in which to wonder what he'd gotten himself into when he'd agreed to this family retreat.

Chapter Four

It wasn't a long drive from the resort to the airport, so Maggie and Garrett were able to fill the time with talk of last night's birthday party. They kept the conversation light and humorous, focused on the girls. She'd worried a bit about this being awkward since she and Garrett had never actually been alone before, but she was quite comfortable with him and he seemed to feel the same way.

She still wasn't entirely sure what had made the girls suggest this outing. Garrett had offered her a way out when he'd reminded his daughters that she had to work on weekday afternoons. All she'd have had to do was say that she was much too busy now—which she was, actually—and they'd have vaguely agreed to get together some other time. That most likely would have been the end of it. But it had sounded like fun, so she'd been honest about being able to take an extra hour off. She hoped Garrett hadn't felt obligated to follow through, though he'd seemed sincere when he'd told her he would enjoy taking her up.

The small airport was busier than she'd expected on a weekday afternoon. Garrett parked in front of a blue metal building in a space marked with a Reserved sign. "The clientele here is mostly general aviation—private owners with small planes. It's a little busy this afternoon because many of the owners are leaving town for the holiday weekend, and others are coming in to spend the Independence Day weekend with relatives in this area."

"Does that make it inconvenient for us to go up this afternoon?"

He unbuckled his seatbelt. "Not at all. Our office is closed today, so our training planes are available. I called my partner just to be sure, but she's not coming in."

The sign over the entrance door of the metal building read Cowherd-McHale Aviation. Maggie raised her eyebrows. "I didn't realize you were a partner in the business."

"I bought in after I got out of the air force last year. My plan had been to serve another four years minimum to qualify for retirement pay, but I thought the girls needed more security than I could give them in the service. I'd already done two short tours in the Middle East and there was always a chance I'd get sent back or reassigned to another base. Sherri Cowherd is an old friend of mine and we figured we could make a decent living giving private lessons and flying charters. We bought out a couple of guys who'd decided to retire, so we had an existing client base to start with, and we're able to swap off hours to give us time with our families. It's worked out well enough so far."

She couldn't help wondering what his relationship was like with his partner. She hadn't heard the girls mention Sherri Cowherd, so apparently she wasn't a big part of their life. When Garrett had mentioned Sherri's family, did he mean that his partner was married or had kids of her own? Not that it was any of her business, of course.

"Do you like your work now?" she asked, tagging after him toward a group of small planes secured to pads.

"Do I like it well enough to enjoy coming to work every day? Sure. Do I sometimes wish I was still in the military? Yes. But my girls come first."

Once again she found herself hoping his daughters would eventually understand the sacrifices he had made for them. They were too young now, and more focused on the rules he set for them than the things he'd given up for them.

She watched in fascination while he did the preflight check outside the little high-wing two-seater. She wasn't really worried about going up in it, but she had to admit it looked awfully tiny sitting there on the tarmac. And then Garrett smiled at her, slipped a pair of aviator sunglasses on his nose and asked, "Ready?"

Feeling her knees melt a little, she thought it was entirely possible that she'd follow him just about anywhere. She cleared her throat. "Um, yes, sure."

He opened the passenger door for her and helped her in. Did his hand linger a bit longer than necessary at the small of her back, or was that just her overwrought imagination? Whichever, it certainly took her mind off her nerves about takeoff.

She couldn't stop watching him as he went through the preflight check inside the plane, taxied onto the runway and accelerated into takeoff. He kept her informed about what he was doing, a hint of the flight instructor in his voice. An air of confidence surrounded him, making it clear that this was little different to him than driving a car. And he looked so darned sexy that her toes curled in the sandals she'd worn with slim-fit jeans and her prettiest top.

He glanced at her when they were in the air. "Doing okay?"

"It's great. The girls were right, the scenery is so much prettier from a small plane than a big commercial airliner."

"I should take you up in an aerobatic plane sometime. Show you the view from upside down."

She laughed, though she wasn't entirely sure he was joking. "Can you fly aerobatic planes?"

Slanting her a crooked smile, he drawled, "Sweetheart, I can fly anything that lifts off the ground."

Seriously. Was the man *trying* to seduce her? Because she was one quirk of his lips away from begging him to park this thing somewhere and fly her instead.

"So, do you want to try it?"

She blinked. "Um—what?"

"The controls." He nodded toward the wheel in front of her. "Want to drive?"

"Oh. Yes, I'd love to."

For the next half hour, he demonstrated what a skilled and patient instructor he was. By the time she turned the controls back over, sat back in her seat and contented herself with admiring the view of the lake and the surrounding area, she felt as though she had a good idea of what went into piloting the little craft. Certainly she couldn't do so on her own after that one brief lesson, but it seemed like something she could conceivably learn to do—with the right instructor, of course. She wondered how much she'd have had to pay for that lesson he'd just given her. Maybe she should consider getting her license, she mused half-seriously.

"You're a good instructor," she told him, speaking over the growl of the engine.

He smiled. "You're a good student."

"I bet you have some interesting stories to tell about some of the lessons you've given."

"I do, at that."

"How long have you wanted to fly?"

"Since I could walk," he replied simply. "Mom did her best to talk me out of it, but my dad flew in Vietnam and he let me take lessons when I was a teenager. He thought maybe I'd get tired of it. I never did."

"I remember your dad, a little. He checked my vision when I was in fifth grade. My best friend got glasses, and I wanted some, too, so I told my mom I couldn't see the board at school. Dr. McHale tested my vision and assured me it was perfect. When I acted disappointed, he told me that not everyone could brag about having perfect vision. By the time I left, I was so proud of my perfect vision that I was no longer envious of my friend's cute new glasses."

Garrett nodded. "That sounds like my dad. He went to optometry school on the G.I. Bill after Vietnam, and he practiced until he died in a car accident almost ten years ago."

"I remember that, too. I think my parents went to his funeral."

"A lot of people came. Mom was pleased that so many turned out to honor him."

He banked the plane into a turn and she was distracted for a moment by looking almost straight down through her side window.

"Speaking of lessons, are you going to teach tennis at the club again?" Garrett asked once they were level again.

Drawing her gaze back into the cockpit, she shook her head. "I was just filling in as a favor to Bill. I'm hardly an expert, but I was the closest he had available on short notice when his regular instructor had to take a few weeks off. I played on a mixed-doubles team in college, so he figured I was qualified."

"The girls thought you were a great teacher."

She smiled wryly. "We had a lot of fun, but I don't plan to make a second career of it."

"See the landing strip ahead?"

She leaned forward. "Yes, I see it."

"We're starting our descent now."

A few minutes later they were on the ground. She watched as Garrett topped off the tank, then secured the plane onto the pad. He stretched a bit to secure one of the wing tie-downs, and muscles rippled beneath his cool clothes. A low sound of appreciation escaped her before she could swallow it.

Garrett glanced over his shoulder. "Did you say something?"

"Um, no. Just clearing my throat." Turning quickly to hide her flushed cheeks, she focused intently on a small jet taking off from the runway.

He chocked the wheels of the Cessna, then approached her again, brushing off his hands on his jeans. That motion almost drew her gaze back to his sturdy thighs, but she managed to keep her eyes on his face. Hardly a hardship.

"Ready to go?

"Yes." On an impulse that overpowered her attempt at keeping a safe distance between them, she laid a hand on his arm. "Thank you so much for taking me up, Garrett. I had such a good time."

He hesitated only a moment, then covered her hand with his own before she could pull it away. His eyes locked with hers, and his voice was just a little husky when he said, "So did I."

She should have drawn back then, but she lingered, savoring the feel of his work-roughened hand on hers. Just for a few moments longer, she promised herself. "I probably shouldn't have taken you away from your family vacation."

His mouth twisted. "To be honest, I enjoyed that part. I love my family and it's great to have this time with them—but it's kind of nice to have a little break from them, too."

She couldn't help laughing, though a bit breathlessly. "I'm picturing myself spending a week in a cabin with my grandparents and parents. I'm crazy about all of them, but I think I'd have to make a break for it at some point."

He nodded. "Sounds like you do understand."

"Absolutely."

They stood there a moment, smiling at each other until their smiles suddenly faded and the sparks of awareness between them threatened to fully ignite. Maggie was pretty sure she wasn't imagining the mutual heat. The possibility that Garrett could be as attracted to her as she was to him changed things considerably between them.

She drew back her hand, shoved it into her pocket and told herself her palm wasn't really still tingling from that all-too-brief contact.

He opened the passenger door of his SUV for her, waited until she'd climbed in, then closed the door and rounded the front. She watched him, admiring the way he moved. The way he looked. Everything about him, darn it.

She could be in a little trouble here.

"Are you in a rush to get back?" Garrett asked as he drove out of the airport.

She probably should be, she thought—but she was in no hurry at all to end this outing. "No, why?"

"Would you mind if we stop by my house on the way? I'd like to collect the mail and check on things."

"I wouldn't mind at all."

"Thanks. It won't take long."

"That's okay. I don't have any reason to hurry home."

Her plans for the evening involved nothing more than laundry and maybe some sewing. No reason to rush back for either.

Garrett and his daughters lived in a tidy redbrick ranch-style house on a quiet street. He pointed to a house across the street, explaining that his mother and grandmother had resided there for many years. The one he was in now had just happened to become available a few weeks before he'd moved back with the girls, so he'd bought it after only a cursory consideration.

"Would you like to come in?" he offered as he parked in the driveway. "I have some sodas if you'd like a cold drink. Or I'll be only a few minutes if you'd rather wait out here."

"Actually, a glass of cold water sounds good."

"I can provide that, too." He opened his door and she did the same.

It was no surprise to Maggie that the house was immaculate and efficiently organized. Garrett's military background showed here as well as in his posture. She might have predicted a neutral, almost sterile decorating style, but instead found that he'd selected warm, comfortable furnishings in rich colors. The kitchen was fitted with top-of-the-line stainless-steel appliances. "Do you cook?" she asked him after accepting a glass of iced water.

Glancing through a stack of mail, he nodded absently. "With two growing girls in the house, I pretty much have to. Basics, mostly. Broiled or grilled meats and fish, roasted or steamed vegetables, lots of salads. I don't like to fry and I'm not very good at baking, but we get by. Mom still likes to cook, so we have dinner together fairly often. Occasionally the girls nag me into ordering pizza, but I'm not a fan of most takeout foods."

She leaned an elbow against a spotless white-tile counter and asked, "So how is a kitten going to fit into your tidy household?"

He chuckled and tossed the mail into a basket on a built-in kitchen desk. "I'm assuming it will be an interesting experience. I'm going to ask the shelter worker to recommend a quiet, well-behaved young cat and hope Kix falls in love with it."

Maggie shook her head. "You just know she'll choose a hyper, curious and mischievous kitten."

"I'd better pick up a large bottle of aspirin on our way to the shelter," Garrett muttered, looking like he was only half joking.

She laughed. "Might not be a bad idea."

He shifted his weight and her amusement faded. She hadn't realized quite how near he'd stood to her. Or had he just moved closer? By accident or intentionally?

He shifted again and suddenly there was more room

between them. His jaw was tight now, his eyes dark. "We should go."

She set her empty water glass on the counter. "Yes."

She hadn't expected her voice to emerge so regretful that even she could hear the reluctance.

Garrett went still, his gaze locked with hers. "Maggie—"

She cleared her throat, wondering why it felt suddenly dry despite the water she'd just swallowed. "Yes?"

"We should go."

"You just said that."

But neither of them moved.

She jumped a good inch when his cell phone buzzed suddenly. He must have been startled, too—a muttered curse escaped him before he glanced at the screen, then answered the call. "Mom? Is something wrong?…Oh. Yeah, sure.…No, go ahead. I'll see you in a while."

"Is everything okay?" Maggie asked when he slipped the phone back into his pocket.

"Yeah. The girls are hungry so they're eating dinner early. Mom said she'd save me a plate, or she suggested I might want to eat out with you if we're in no hurry to get back to the resort."

"Oh."

"So. We should go back."

She couldn't help laughing again, though somewhat breathlessly this time. "I'm getting that idea."

He grimaced wryly. "Maybe I've said it before."

"Once or twice."

A faint sigh escaped him. "It's just that—well, you've probably figured out that I find you very attractive."

She shouldn't have been particularly surprised by his candor, considering what she knew of him. Still, she couldn't help being caught unaware by his words.

She felt her pulse rate speed up in response to his unexpected admission. "You do? I mean, I wondered—"

He took another half step backward, putting just a little more safe distance between them. "I'm trying to tell you that you don't have to worry about me getting out of line. I don't want to cause any discomfort between us."

For some reason the more self-conscious the usually composed Garrett became, the more at ease Maggie felt. And the more attractive she found him, which was hard to imagine, considering how strongly she was drawn to him. "I appreciate your chivalry."

He frowned. "You're laughing at me."

"I'm laughing at both of us," she admitted. "I've wondered if you could see how attracted I am to you."

He looked at her for a moment, then said very distinctly, "Well, damn."

A soft, husky chuckle escaped her. "I'm not sure how to interpret that."

"You and me—not a good idea, Maggie. Even if there weren't any other issues between us, the timing is all wrong for me to even consider getting involved. With anyone."

She shrugged, both amused and flattered by his uncharacteristic awkwardness. She couldn't help but be curious about those other "issues," but she wasn't going to argue with him. Not when there were so many other things she would rather do with him. "I'm not looking to get seriously involved, either. That isn't why I let the girls talk me into this outing with you."

"Then why did you?"

"Because I wanted to see the resort from a small plane," she answered lightly. "And because I thought we could both use a couple hours of relaxation without our families around."

And because the thought of being alone with him in an enclosed space had been incredibly appealing, she could have added.

He pushed a hand through his short, crisp hair and gave a little huff of a laugh. "You got that right."

A quick rush of sympathy drew her thoughts momentarily away from her physical responses to him. "Do you ever get time away from work or your family?"

"Not very often. When I'm not working, it seems like the girls always have something going. School activities or dance or music lessons or dentist appointments or birthday parties they have to be chauffeured to. Or Mom's car has a flat or one of her appliances won't work or she needs lightbulbs changed that she can't reach or one of her faucets is dripping or..."

He stopped with a grimace and a shake of his head. "Sorry. Didn't mean to go on a self-pity rant. I love my family and I take care of them because I choose to."

"I understand. You're talking to someone who lives within a stone's throw of most of my extended family," she reminded him. "Sometimes I just need to escape for some me time. Sounds like you could use some more of that yourself."

"I run almost every day for an hour or so early in the mornings before I get the girls up for breakfast. Sometimes Jay and I play golf or watch a ball game when the girls have other plans. But you're probably right. I do need to get out more."

A runner. She should have known he did something strenuous to stay in such great shape. Which brought her attention right back around to how appealing he was to her, and to his confession that he felt the same way about her. She moved a step closer to him, speaking in a low voice. "You should definitely make time for yourself. Just for fun."

He leaned against the bar, looking somewhat more relaxed again. "Fun, huh?"

"Absolutely," she said, holding his gaze. "No responsibilities, no taking care of anyone else, no watching what you say or do. Just totally selfish fun, for at least a few hours at a time. When's the last time you did that?"

He made a face. "It's been a while."

At least a year, she'd bet. Since he'd become fully accountable for two young girls. "When's the last time you acted purely on impulse?"

"Probably even longer."

"That's what I thought." On an impish whim, she stepped even closer and took his face in her hands. And then planted a smacking kiss right on his nicely shaped mouth. Just because she wanted to.

Garrett looked startled but not displeased by her move. One side of his mouth kicked up into a slight smile when she drew back an inch. "I never thought you were the type to play with fire, Maggie."

She chuckled softly, her heart racing now in response to that all-too-brief kiss. "I've been known to scorch my fingertips a few times."

His hands settled at her hips before she could move away. "My fingers are still feeling a little cold."

What the hell. She wrapped her arms around his neck, momentarily abandoning caution. "Then maybe we should heat them up."

"Maybe we should." He settled his mouth against hers, their smiles meeting then melding into a kiss hot enough to scorch much more than her fingertips. She felt the heat surging all the way through her, simmering deep inside her. This buttoned-down, ex-military single dad definitely knew how to kiss.

Finally releasing her mouth, he drew his head back just far enough so he could look into her eyes. He didn't release her, nor did she remove her arms from around his neck. It felt so good right where she was, pressed again his lean, muscled form, wrapped in the warmth that radiated from him.

"You've managed to surprise me," he said, his voice just a little rough-edged now. "That doesn't happen very often."

Lacing her fingers behind his head, she lifted an eyebrow. "What surprises you? That I'm attracted to you? Or that I admitted it? I'm not really a game player when it comes to this sort of thing. I would have kept my interest to myself if you hadn't said something, but since we've both made it clear that we're not looking to complicate our lives any more than they already are, there's no reason we can't be honest."

"I'm a fan of honesty."

She laughed softly. "So am I."

"Even when it stings," he added with a grimace that made her suspect he associated a bad memory with brutal honesty. Something told her it had to do with his ex-wife, but that wasn't something she particularly wanted to get into.

Though she'd avoided the complications of marriage and children to this point, she'd had her share of romantic disappointments. She had seen her sister survive a bad marriage and move on to a much happier life. The past was past, in her opinion. No need to dwell on it.

"Even then." She took a quick nip of his lower lip, then dropped her arms with a slight sigh and stepped back. "So what's on the agenda now?"

"I should probably get back to the family," he said, tugging at the open collar of his shirt as if it had suddenly tried to close on him.

Maggie shook her head in exasperation. This man really needed to learn how to take a few hours for himself. His family had even called him to encourage him to do so.

"Okay, here's the deal," she said brusquely. "I'm buying you dinner. It's the least I can do after you took me for that lovely flight. It's still early, so you'll be back in plenty of time to spend a little while with your family before bedtime."

His left eyebrow shot upward. "Doesn't sound like I have much choice."

"You have no choice at all," she assured him. "I'm totally kidnapping you. That way you don't have to feel guilty."

"I don't feel guilty for having dinner away from the kids every once in a while," he said, an edge of defensiveness to his voice.

She merely looked at him.

He sighed. "Well, I try not to, anyway."

She caught his wrist and gave a tug. "Okay, consider yourself my prisoner. I'll release you only after you've eaten a leisurely meal accompanied by adult conversation, a glass of wine and servers dressed in anything other than clown costumes."

The expression that briefly crossed his face almost made her grin. She might have described it as wistful. "Sounds pretty nice," he conceded.

"Let's go, McHale."

"Since you're giving me no other choice…" Chuckling, he followed her out of his house, locking the doors behind them.

* * *

Maggie looked even prettier than usual in the flickering glow of candlelight. It brought out the streaks of honey in her wavy brown hair and made her hazel eyes glow. Her sun-kissed fair skin looked flawless and invitingly soft. Having so recently held her in his arms, Garrett knew that to be a fair assessment.

"Tell me about your work," he encouraged her over appetizers in the little lakeside Italian restaurant she'd chosen. "Did you choose to toil in the family business or did you feel pressured into it?"

As soon as the question left his lips, he wondered if he'd worded it a bit too bluntly, but she didn't seem to mind his curiosity. She cut into a stuffed mushroom with her fork as she answered.

"A little of both, I suppose. It was always just assumed that we'd work in the resort after college, though we were never actually ordered to do so. Shelby was always the most enthusiastic about it. She loves the bookkeeping and true business end of the company. She and Aaron will undoubtedly take over someday, though it will be several years before the generation above us is ready to step down, of course. Steven is off pursuing his dream of fighting forest fires, but maybe he'll come back someday and resume his place in upper management. Hannah will probably be content to handle the marketing from Dallas and sit in on regular family board meetings while she raises Claire and any other children she and Andrew may have. As for Lori—"

She shrugged at the mention of her young cousin who'd recently eloped to California with a rebellious musician. "Who knows if she'll ever be back? Maybe if she and Zach split up, which most of the family considers inevitable, she'll want to come home."

"And what about you? You don't want to compete with Shelby and Aaron to take over the whole operation?" He kept his tone teasing, but he was genuinely curious about her ambitions for her future.

"Me?" She laughed and shook her head. "No secret desire for power here. I'm perfectly content to let the parents and the cousins rule the resort."

"Upper management doesn't interest you?"

"Stress, headaches, worries about weather, insurance and liabilities, government regulations, taxes?" She made a show of shuddering delicately. "No, thank you. Supervising my staff gives me all the challenge I desire. I hire judiciously to minimize the problems as much as possible, but we still have the occasional drama or staff shortage or other personnel problems."

Garrett doubted that Maggie dealt with an excessive amount of drama among her staff. From what he'd observed, the workers she'd hired were cheerful and dedicated. They seemed to like working for her—though he couldn't imagine why they wouldn't—and he suspected they were fairly compensated for their hours. The Bell family was known for their generosity and contributions to local charities, earning a good living for themselves through their hard work but also willing to spread the profits within their community. He knew Jay had advised several members of his congregation to fill out applications for the rare job opening at the resort.

"So, no secret desires to leave the resort and pursue a childhood dream, like your cousin Steven and his firefighting?" he asked lightly.

She shrugged. "I don't have an overwhelming urge to pursue another career. I like the flexibility of working at the resort, so that I'm in charge of setting my own schedule to an extent. I arrange my calendar to give me the freedom to spend a few hours a week at the gym or take the occasional weekend off with friends. There's even more free time during the off-season. This coming winter I'm planning a trip to Jamaica with a couple of friends from college. We haven't nailed down a date yet, but we're thinking sometime in February. I love to travel and hope to do more of it in the future now that things have settled down at the resort."

She certainly seemed to be popular enough with those friends she had mentioned. Though she had silenced the ringer on her cell phone, he'd heard the soft buzz of the vibration feature quite a few times. She glanced at the screen occasionally—presumably making sure none of the calls were emergencies—but didn't answer, giving her full attention to their conversation. He appreciated that courtesy.

It didn't sound as if she was in any hurry to settle down with a husband and kids. As young as she was, she had plenty of time for those things. He couldn't blame her for wanting to enjoy her freedom while she was young and single, something he'd never really done. Despite the mistake he'd made in marrying too young and too impulsively, he couldn't regret the outcome, wouldn't trade his girls for any measure of carefree independence.

Something she'd said suddenly struck him. "You said things have settled down at the resort?"

She smiled wryly and reached for her wineglass. "The past couple of years were a little stressful, to say the least. I don't know how much you've heard...?"

He shrugged. "Not a lot. I heard talk about some arrests being made last year, but that was just about the time I was settling here with the girls, so I didn't get a lot of details."

She leaned back a bit to allow their server to quietly slip their meals in place on the table. After declining a wine refill, she resumed the conversation. "It all started with Hannah's ex-husband—or as he's known in the family, the evil ex. We'd just started to recover from the economic downturn a couple years ago when her ex started threatening lawsuits against the resort for breach of promises he said we'd made when he joined the family and went to work for the resort. I use the term *work* loosely in his case, since he never put a lot of effort into any of the various positions he decided to sample. He claimed to have a prenup that Hannah swore she'd never signed, said he had a paper trail promising him a partnership in the business, that sort of thing."

Garrett grimaced. "Extortion?"

"Pretty much," she agreed. "It got so bad that Dad and Uncle C.J. decided to bring in an investigator to check out the threat. That's how we met Andrew Walker, who works for his family's investigation and security firm in Dallas."

"Andrew who is now married to Hannah," Garrett said to prove he was following along. "And the identical twin brother to your cousin Shelby's husband, Aaron."

She smiled. "Yes. Hannah and Andrew met almost two years ago when Andrew started investigating the evil ex. It wasn't the most auspicious beginning to their relationship, but they fell in love anyway. They just didn't admit it, even to themselves, until almost a year later, when Hannah was pregnant with Claire. But that's another story."

A story that sounded interesting in itself, but Garrett let it go. "So Andrew was able to debunk the evil ex's claims?"

Chuckling at his use of the derogatory nickname,

Maggie nodded in satisfaction. "Not only that, he found rock-solid proof that Wade had embezzled funds from the resort before he and Hannah split and that he'd forged checks and purchase orders. Not only did Wade fail at bankrupting us, as he was trying to do, he served time for fraud and embezzlement. He got out last month, but last I heard, he's left the state. I can't imagine he would attempt to bother any of us again."

Garrett wound pasta around his fork. "I wouldn't think so."

"Then last June some moron tried to set up a stolen-goods fencing operation out of cabin seven...."

He looked up with a lifted eyebrow. "Seriously?"

"Yes. Shelby suspected something was going on and asked Aaron to help her look into it. Aaron was here for nothing more than a vacation and didn't even work for his family's investigation agency, but she figured he'd been exposed to the P.I. business enough to qualify," she explained with a laugh.

Having known Shelby for a few months now, Garrett wasn't particularly surprised by the somewhat convoluted logic.

"Anyway, they uncovered the operation—during which the scumbag held Shelby at knifepoint for several hours hoping to use her as a hostage so he could escape." Her faint shudder was entirely genuine this time, and he could tell the memories of her cousin's ordeal still troubled her.

"Aaron was able to rescue her without anyone getting hurt," she went on. "But needless to say it was a traumatic experience for Shelby and for the rest of the family—especially when it was followed only days later by Hannah being stalked by one of the evil ex's dumped girlfriends. The woman was emotionally disturbed, and she blamed Hannah for Wade's arrest. She slashed Hannah's tires, sabotaged her porch so that Hannah could have been injured in a fall while six months pregnant and threw a rock through a window where Hannah and Andrew were standing."

"Wow."

"During the same period, Steven broke his leg in a mowing accident and announced that he was leaving to train in firefighting, and Lori quit college and ran off to marry a guy her parents disapproved of, and then Hannah married Andrew and moved to Dallas with him and the baby. Fortunately the past six months have been busy but uneventful, which is the way the family tends to prefer things."

"As do you?"

She smiled. "Absolutely. The quieter it is at work, the fewer responsibilities fall on me, which makes it easier to slip away for me time."

Someone who didn't know better might think Maggie wasn't a conscientious, hardworking member of the Bell Resort team. Despite her teasing self-deprecation, Garrett did know better. "I think you mentioned me time earlier."

"It's very important," she assured him gravely, though her eyes danced in the candlelight. "I highly recommend it. Even for a busy single dad."

He took a sip of his wine and returned the glass to the table. "I'm certainly enjoying this evening. As much as I like spending time with my daughters, it's nice to eat a meal without having to tell Kix to stop talking for a minute to breathe. Or chew."

Maggie gave a little laugh. "She does like to talk."

"Yes, she does."

"So when's the last time you went out to see a film that wasn't animated or featured talking animals?"

He frowned as he tried to remember the last time he'd sat in a theater that wasn't filled with babbling kids and crying babies. "It's been a while."

"That new summer blockbuster spy film premieres next week. Not an intellectual film, but not a kids' movie, either. Want to check it out with me?"

He felt his left eyebrow rise a fraction. Was she asking him out again?

Maggie giggled at whatever she saw in his expression. "It's part of my campaign to loosen you up and teach you about me time. Or I guess technically it's you time. No strings, no expectations, just a couple of single adults having fun together. If you like, of course."

"I like," he said, his voice just a little husky to his own ears. He stuffed his mouth full of pasta to keep himself from following up with something stupid. He was way out of practice when it came to flirtation. How long had it been since an attractive young woman had so casually asked him out? Not counting the man-hungry mama at Kix's birthday party, of course.

No strings, no expectations. Maggie had made it clear she wasn't looking for a relationship with him—no surprise since she had plans for travel and fun that didn't include a ready-made family. But he wasn't looking to add anyone else to his already hectic household, either. A summer fling—even if only a couple of dates—sounded like exactly what he needed right now. And he couldn't think of anyone he'd rather spend those evenings with than pretty Maggie Bell, until her attention inevitably moved on from this impulsive project of teaching a harried single dad about me time.

Chapter Five

All in all, Maggie was quite satisfied with the outcome of her brazen commandeering of the evening. Behind the wheel of his SUV, Garrett looked more relaxed than she'd seen him—well, pretty much since she'd first met him. He was smiling, even gave a sexy rumble of laughter occasionally. They had lingered over dessert without talking about either of their families, their topics centered instead on books, music, local politics—an adult conversation he seemed to enjoy as much as she did.

She had no doubt that he looked forward to returning to his family retreat at the resort, that he was enjoying the time with his children, his mother and his grandmother, but he'd needed the brief respite from them, too. There had to be a satisfactory compromise between his late ex-wife's continuous escape from her responsibility to her children—at least, from what Maggie had surmised—and Garrett's totally selfless dedication to them. It was no hardship for her to volunteer to give Garrett an occasional glimpse of his options. It wasn't as if he had no one to help with the girls, or had to leave them with paid chaperones. His mother was perfectly capable and obviously willing to spend time with them.

His phone buzzed just as he drove into the resort. It was still early evening and the sun had not yet set, though long shadows were beginning to spread across the grounds.

Garrett braked at the side of the road to answer the call. "I just drove through the gate, Mom. I'll be— What? When did you see her last?"

Maggie didn't like the sound of that question. She swiveled in her seat to watch his face. The relaxation was gone now, replaced by stern lines around his eyes and mouth. He didn't look so much worried as annoyed, she decided in relief.

"I'll find her," he promised his mother. "I'll be there with her shortly."

"What?" Maggie asked when Garrett shoved his phone back into his pocket.

"Mom let the girls walk down to the shoreline behind the cabin to take pictures of the sunset with Kix's new camera while she cleaned the kitchen. Kix came back inside a few minutes ago. Payton didn't."

She winced. "Did Kix say where Payton went?"

He put the SUV in gear again. "She said Payton decided to take a walk. Kix warned her she should ask first, but Payton wouldn't listen."

"What about her cell phone?" Maggie knew Payton had one because she'd sent and received several texts while they'd decorated yesterday, though Payton had complained that she had to be careful not to go over her allotted number of monthly texts. Apparently her father wouldn't spring for the unlimited texting plan that "all the other kids" had.

"Mom said she left it in the cabin, which is a surprise. I was beginning to think it was permanently attached to her hand."

Maggie peered out the front window, looking for a glimpse of Payton as Garrett drove slowly toward the marina. Quite a few guests were still milling around the playground, the pool, the marina and the swimming area on this pleasant summer evening, but she didn't immediately spot Payton among them.

"I'm sure she'll be fine," she said. "The resort really is quite safe."

"Still, she knows better than to run off and worry her grandmother this way. She should have asked permission."

Knowing how protective Paulette was toward her granddaughters, Maggie suspected Payton had avoided asking because she'd figured she would be turned down. Which didn't excuse her behavior, of course, but she could see how a girl in her teens would be inclined to chafe against such close supervision. Maggie and her sister and cousins had always treated the entire resort as their personal backyard, as at home in the campgrounds as in their own living rooms. They'd had rules to follow and curfews to meet, but they hadn't been guarded every waking minute. She knew there were no hard-and-fast guidelines for successful parenting—another reason the very idea struck fear into her heart—but she supposed Garrett and his mom were proceeding as they thought best.

Garrett spotted his daughter first. "There she is."

Following the direction of his nod, Maggie glanced toward the day-use area near the designated swimming beach. Picnic tables, fixed charcoal grills and public restrooms were located in the small park. Three teenage boys and a girl gathered around one of the picnic tables, the girl sitting on the tabletop, the boys jostling and milling around her. Payton was the girl on the table.

She heard what might have been a low growl rumble in Garrett's throat.

"You can let me out here," she said rather too quickly as she motioned toward the main building. "I'll see if Mom needs help closing the store."

Keeping one eye on his daughter, who hadn't yet noticed his arrival, Garrett stopped in front of the building. "I enjoyed spending the day with you, Maggie. I'm sorry it had to end this abruptly."

She couldn't help wondering how their evening might have ended differently had it not been for Payton's rebellion. Would there have been another spontaneous kiss? Or two? A pleasant, if necessarily brief, interlude of acknowledgment of their healthy, mutual attraction?

Maybe it was best that they hadn't had that opportunity, she acknowledged regretfully. As it was, their outing had ended with a practical reminder of the obstacles standing between them when it came to any sort of long-term relationship, even if either of them had been looking for one.

"I understand. It's all part of parenthood, I suppose."

He grunted. "Got to admit, it's not my favorite part."

Just as she reached for her door handle, Garrett asked, "Do you know those boys?"

"I recognize the Ferguson brothers," she said, glancing that way again. "I don't know the other boy."

"He looks older than the Ferguson kids."

"Yes, he does." Maggie figured the guy standing

closest to Payton was at least seventeen. "I haven't seen him before. He must be staying in the campgrounds."

Garrett nodded grimly. "Maybe I'll just go introduce myself to him."

She started again to open the door, then paused. Aware that she was offering assistance that had not been requested, she said carefully, "Um, Garrett? I know you're going to yell at Payton, and I don't blame you because she upset her grandmother—but maybe you'll wait until you're back at the cabin? Girls her age are so easily humiliated."

She was relieved to see that he didn't look any more annoyed by her advice than he'd already been at his daughter's behavior. He merely nodded. "I'll try not to emotionally scar her," he said ironically. "But I want her to know she owes my mom more respect than this."

"Of course. But treating her like a little girl in front of the boys she's trying to impress would probably mortify her more than teach her a lesson. Trust me, I *was* a thirteen-year-old girl and I still cringe at a few memories from that awkward time."

A possible solution occurred to her. "Why don't I go get her for you?" she offered impulsively. "I'll tell her the family's waiting for her to watch a movie or something. That will let her save face and then you can rip into her in private."

Again, she was stepping in where she wasn't sure she was welcome, but he merely shrugged one shoulder. "You're welcome to tag along, but I want to talk to those boys."

Biting her lower lip, Maggie settled back into her seat. She was still tempted to bolt for the sanctuary of the store, but she knew what it was like to be a teenager embarrassed by an overprotective father. She'd had her mother to intercede and make sure her dad didn't overreact. She certainly had no intention of acting as Payton's surrogate mother—but maybe she could be a friend to the girl and defuse this particular situation, at least to an extent.

After that, Payton and Garrett were on their own.

Garrett tried to keep Maggie's advice in mind as they approached the picnic table where Payton giggled and flirted with the three boys. When he saw how close the oldest boy had moved to Payton, it was all he could do not to snarl, yet he made a deliberate effort to keep his expression firm but not murderous. It wasn't easy. This punk wasn't much younger than some of the airmen he'd trained. What the hell was he doing making eyes at a thirteen-year-old girl?

Payton's jaw dropped when she caught sight of them. She glanced frantically at her watch. "Dad? Maggie? Um, you're back earlier than I expected."

He nodded curtly.

Maggie spoke quickly, probably to head off anything embarrassing he might say. "We just got back. You were so right, Payton, I had a great time in the small plane. I can see why you love flying in them so much. Your dad told me you're already quite good at handling the controls."

The boys looked impressed, as Maggie had hoped. Maybe that would ease the sting when Garrett demanded that Payton accompany him home.

Maggie glanced at the Ferguson brothers. "I hope you boys are enjoying your stay with us this week. It's always nice to have you and your family here with us. I don't believe we've met," she said to the older boy. "I'm Maggie Bell. Are you staying in our campgrounds?"

He nodded and muttered, "I'm Stu. My family's camping here a couple days on our way from Baton Rouge to Arizona in an RV. My folks want to see the Grand Canyon. I think it's lame, but you know."

"It's nice to meet you, Stu. Tell your parents to be sure to let us know if there's anything we can do to make your stay better, will you?"

He shrugged. Garrett was not impressed with the lanky kid's manners—or lack thereof. He doubted the boy was the brightest bulb on his family tree.

He started to speak, but once again Maggie overrode him, turning to Payton with a bright smile. "We were just headed to the cabin to visit with the rest of your family a bit when we saw you here. Why don't we give you a ride back?"

Payton tossed back her hair with a sidelong look at the boys shuffling their feet nearby. "I'll be there soon," she promised with an artificial airiness to her voice. "I just want to talk to my new friends a little while longer."

Garrett shook his head. He'd given Maggie her chance, but it was his turn to take over. "*Now,* Payton."

His daughter knew better than to argue with that particular tone, especially in front of her friends, but the look in her eyes told him she would have plenty to say later. Fine with him. He had a few things to say himself.

"Wow," Stu stage-whispered mockingly to the older Ferguson brother, making little effort to keep the adults from hearing. "Wonder if he lets her pee without permission."

Payton flushed. Maggie made a low sound that might have been a groan.

Garrett drew himself into his straightest military-officer posture and eyed the kid through narrowed eyes. "Are you aware that my daughter is only thirteen?"

"Dad," Payton hissed.

Stu cleared his throat, his Adam's apple bobbing a few times in his skinny neck. "Thought she was older," he muttered.

Garrett had no doubt Payton had made no attempt to correct that misconception.

"And how old are *you?*" he inquired coolly.

A mix of defiance, pride and nerves was audible in the mumbled reply. "I'm, uh, seventeen."

Garrett gave him a look that went all the way down past his oversize T-shirt and sagging shorts to his sandaled feet, then back up to his messy hair. "Thought you were younger," he said.

The other boys snickered. Stu's already splotchy face reddened. "I was just being nice to the kids here," he said, shifting away from the younger boys. "I gotta go, got things to do tonight."

"I thought you were going to make s'mores with us later," the youngest boy protested.

"Nah. That's for kids." He turned and shuffled in the opposite direction, his shoulders hunched, movements jerky and irritated. Garrett got the impression that Stu was immature for his age and probably made a habit of hanging out with younger kids to raise his own self-esteem.

He wouldn't be getting an ego boost from thirteen-year-old Payton.

And speaking of Payton, the looks she was shooting at him now could have scorched the skin off his bones if she'd happened to possess laser abilities. "Let's go," he said, motioning toward his SUV.

"I'll see you guys around," she muttered to the Ferguson brothers, then swept past her father without looking at him again.

Giving a short nod to the wide-eyed brothers, Garrett followed her, thinking that this was a really sucky end to what had been a pretty great day. Some might call this a much-needed reality check, for both him and Maggie. He wouldn't soon forget Maggie's expression when she'd hastily asked him to drop her off at the main building. She'd been reluctant to get in the middle of the confrontation—and he couldn't blame her for that. She probably now regretted her knee-jerk offer to intervene on Payton's behalf.

"I'll walk to the cabin," Payton said.

He opened the back passenger door of the SUV. "Get in."

With a sigh that could have blown out a cake's worth of candles, she plopped into the passenger seat and crossed her arms mutinously over her chest. The gesture drew his attention downward and made him scowl. Looked like a shopping trip was in order. Her T-shirt was getting a little small, drawing a bit too much attention to her developing figure. Her grandmother usually took her shopping for clothes and underwear and such; he would arrange another outing next week.

"You know, I just remembered something I need to do back at the office," Maggie said, stepping back. "I'm sure the two of you have things to discuss."

He nodded somberly, both appreciative of her discretion and annoyed by the need for it. "We'll see you later. Thanks again for dinner."

Her smile looked just a bit strained, though she kept her tone light. "Thanks again for the plane ride. Good night, Garrett. Good night, Payton," she added through the car window.

Payton mumbled a barely audible response. Garrett figured she was dreading what was to come—and rightly so.

He had never expected to be solely responsible for two budding teenage girls, he thought as he made the short, tensely silent drive to the cabin. This had not been in his long-term life plan, which had once included a till-death marriage, service in the military until retirement, coparenting his daughters to successful adulthood. He wasn't sure he was at all qualified for doing this on his own, with only the help of his mom—but since he had no other choice, he would continue to do the best he knew how. Which did not include allowing Payton to run unsupervised with three teenage boys, one almost old enough to enlist.

"Hi, Daddy," Kix called out from the sofa when he and Payton entered the cabin. She sat cross-legged with his laptop open in front of her while her grandmother fluttered around the room and her great-grandmother knitted agitatedly. "I'm reading all about taking care of cats. We should take the aloe vera plant out of the kitchen. Aloe vera can make kitties sick if they eat it. Did you have fun with Maggie? Is Payton in a lot of trouble for going off without asking Grammy's permission?"

"Butt out, Kix," Payton snarled.

"You're the one who ruined everything," Kix shot back to her sister.

Garrett wasn't sure what Kix meant by that, but his mother interrupted then to read Payton the riot act about worrying her sick by running off without permission. He didn't intercede until his mom began to list all the terrible things that could have happened—drowning, kidnapping, run down by a car, attacked by wild animals. As the options grew increasingly less reasonable, he finally stepped in to say, "Pull a stunt like that again, Payton, and the vacation is over."

She looked as though she was tempted to stamp her foot, but she knew better. "I was just talking to some other kids," she protested fiercely. "I wasn't doing anything wrong."

"You know exactly what you did wrong," he countered. "Grammy asked you not to leave without telling her, and you did it anyway. You frightened her and you upset Meemaw and that is unacceptable. When I leave you in Grammy's care, I expect you to follow her instructions to the letter, is that clear?"

"Grammy never lets me do anything," Payton wailed. "She treats me like a little kid. You all do. I'm *thirteen!*"

He hated seeing the look of hurt cross his mother's face. But something in his daughter's expression was just as disturbing for him. Did Payton really feel so stifled and misunderstood? As much as he disliked the very idea, she really hadn't been doing anything all that bad by talking to a few boys in a very public place. But neither could he allow her the impression that it was acceptable for her to ignore her grandmother's rules.

"I did offer you the opportunity to go up in the plane with Maggie and me," he reminded her. "You chose to stay here, knowing who would be in charge."

"And I didn't forbid you and Kix to go down to the lakeside unsupervised when you asked," his mother added in a wounded voice. "All I requested was that you stay near the cabin so I wouldn't worry."

"You always worry," Payton muttered, looking at her grandmother through her eyelashes. "I love you a lot, Grammy, but even Maggie's grandmother said you're a worrywart."

Garrett almost groaned at that. Predictably, Esther

stiffened in her chair, her chin shooting upward. "Dixie Bell has no business criticizing our family to you, Payton. I'm tempted to go find her right now and give her a big slice of what for."

Grimacing with the realization of what she'd ignited with her thoughtless comment, Payton said, "She wasn't really criticizing, Meemaw. She was sort of joking. But it's kind of true, anyway. Grammy does worry a lot. You've said so yourself."

"I can say whatever I want about my own daughter," her great-grandmother replied regally. "Dixie, on the other hand, has no call to go poking her big nose into our business."

Garrett happened to glance toward Kix, who was biting her lower lip and looking anxiously from one angry family member to another. He sighed and pushed a hand through his hair. "Okay, let's drop it for now. Payton, apologize to your grandmother for worrying her and we'll let it go with that. This time."

"I'm sorry, Grammy," she murmured, looking down at her feet.

Her grandmother nodded, though she didn't look completely appeased. "We'll drop it for now. Let's bring out the milk and the cookies we made this afternoon and we'll have dessert."

"Could we play Settlers of Catan?" Kix asked hopefully, so obviously eager to put the unpleasantness behind them and start having fun again.

Though Garrett wasn't really in the mood for a board game, he agreed for Kix's sake. He might as well distract himself with the family interaction; it would keep him from mentally replaying those too-few kisses with Maggie. At least until he went to bed alone that night and had nothing to do but stare at the darkened ceiling and remember how it felt to hold pretty, unobtainable Maggie Bell in his arms. He'd bet now she was rethinking her suggestion that they should see a movie together on another pleasant, no-strings, all-adult outing.

Because she felt a little guilty about taking off early the afternoon before, even though she'd made sure her work was completed first, Maggie put a little extra effort into Thursday's chores. She was on the run all day, as were the rest of the family and staff. Additional weekend guests had been pouring in since early that morning in campers and pickups and minivans. The swimming area was crowded, picnic tables full, the long-reserved pavilion jostling with a big family reunion that had been planned for more than a year. The whole resort was abuzz with excitement about the evening's planned fireworks display that would be set off from a barge on the lake. They had sponsored fireworks in the past, but this would be the biggest display yet. Maggie looked forward to it herself.

She handled two minicrises during the morning. Her newest staff member, Darby Burns, passed out while cleaning. It turned out the too-conscientious novice worker had neglected to properly hydrate on this very warm July Fourth. Because Maggie had stressed self-pacing and regular hydration breaks, she was almost as exasperated as she was concerned by Darby's neglect of herself. A cold cloth and a big glass of iced water combined with a fifteen-minute break did the trick. Maggie offered Darby the rest of the day off with regular pay, but Darby insisted she was able to get back to work. She seemed humiliated to have caused a scene, and was eager to turn the attention away from herself.

The second issue of the morning came when a guest

called to report that she'd shattered a bottle of a particularly pungent perfume in her motel room. The scent was overpowering, the woman added without apology. Would the maids please take care of it while the woman and her husband went for a long bicycle ride? Because Maggie's staff had dealt with much worse things to clean up, they were able to handle this spill efficiently, leaving the aired-out room smelling much fresher than they'd found it. Just par for the course in resort housekeeping.

"I thought you smelled a little more flowery than usual," Shelby teased when she and Maggie shared sandwiches and sodas for a late lunch that afternoon. The diner had been packed with holiday guests and neither Shelby nor Maggie wanted to take time to go back to their houses, so they'd grabbed sandwiches from downstairs and hidden out in Shelby's upstairs office to eat them.

Having just told her cousin about the eventful morning, Maggie chuckled and washed down a bite of turkey and provolone on whole wheat with a sip of diet soda. "You can't imagine how bad that room smelled when we first walked in. Nearly knocked us backward. That is some powerful perfume, even when it's not a whole bottle's worth."

"Yuck. I hate perfume, anyway. Never wear the stuff."

Maggie chuckled. "I know. I rarely do, either. Got out of the habit when I was dating Nathan. Remember how his eyes would swell shut whenever he was around something that triggered his allergies?"

"Poor guy, so many things did. I liked him. Haven't heard you mention him in a while. Do you ever hear from him?"

"He calls occasionally just to chat," Maggie replied offhandedly. "He's seeing someone fairly seriously now. An immunologist."

Shelby giggled. "Sounds reasonable."

Maggie and Nathan had dated for several months a couple of years earlier, until they had mutually acknowledged that while they liked each other very much, the sparks just weren't there for anything long-term. They hadn't broken up so much as they'd just drifted apart, no drama or tears involved. Her few relationships all seemed to end that way: pleasant, amiable, maybe a little disappointing, but not heartbreaking.

She wanted to believe the same would be true if she spent a little time with Garrett prior to her planned trip to Jamaica. They could occasionally have fun, flirt, enjoy each other's company, savor the escapes from work and family and still part on friendly terms when the time came, since neither of them expected anything more. Right?

Shelby had always been far too intuitive. Maybe that was why she commented just then, "So, I heard you went flying with Garrett McHale yesterday."

Maggie nodded around a bite of sandwich. After swallowing, she said lightly, "Yes, he took me up in a two-seater plane after I told him I'd never been in one. It was fun. We flew over the resort and I loved seeing the place from the air. He even let me take the controls, which was so cool."

"Sounds like fun."

"It really was."

"He always seems so serious on Sunday mornings. Pleasant, but very reserved."

"Ex-military," Maggie said with a shrug. "He planned to retire from there until he became fully responsible for his daughters. But underneath that air-force-major exterior, he's really quite funny and nice."

Shelby lifted an eyebrow. "Is he?"

"Yes, he is."

Her cousin propped her elbow on her desk, cradled her chin in her palm and studied her with curiosity. "Some interest there?"

"Do I find him sexy as all get-out? Yes. Am I expecting anything serious to develop? No."

"How come?"

"You know me, Shel. I don't do serious."

"Well, I know you haven't to this point, but I thought maybe someday…?"

Maggie shrugged and crumpled the empty sandwich wrapper into a ball. "Who knows? But not now. And definitely not with a single dad of two adolescent daughters."

"You seem fond of the girls."

"They're great. Bright, enthusiastic, funny. But Payton is just getting into the teen-rebellion stage and Kix isn't far away from it herself, and that scares the living daylights out of me."

"Probably scares Garrett, too," Shelby remarked ironically.

Maggie gave a short laugh. "Yeah. I think it does."

"Has to be tough for him, but at least he has help from his mother and grandmother."

Maggie nodded. "I'm sure he's grateful for them."

She couldn't help thinking, though, that his mother was a little overwhelmed, considering her age and the fact that she'd raised only one quiet and well-behaved son. Suddenly dealing with a pair of hormonal teenage girls had to be a shock for her. As for Garrett's acerbic grandmother…well, suffice it to say she wasn't much help.

Shelby gave a little sigh and began to clean up the mess from their office picnic. "I guess all the weddings in the family lately—including mine—have got weddings on my mind. I know Mimi's already been throwing pretty pointed hints your way, so I won't pile on."

Chuckling, Maggie nodded. "I appreciate that."

Their grandmother had been unable to resist pointing out at each recent opportunity that Maggie was now her only unmarried granddaughter. She thought Maggie, at twenty-seven, should be giving serious consideration to settling down and starting her own family rather than spending weekends with groups of friends and planning trips to exotic locations. "You could always see Jamaica on a honeymoon," she had hinted broadly.

"At least Mimi won't be trying to throw me at Garrett," she said with a grin. "She would never want to fix me up with Esther Lincoln's grandson. It's bad enough in her opinion that I'm even friendly with the family."

Shelby winked at her. "Yet another reason for you to be friendly with them. It's always kind of fun to poke at Mimi, isn't it?"

Maggie laughed. As much as they loved their grandmother, there were times when the younger generation enjoyed pulling her chain a bit. Mimi was so bluntly outspoken and opinionated, not above getting in a few little digs herself. "There is that."

Pushing back her chair, Shelby stood. "I'd better go down and help out. It's crazy down there. Your mom's been running back and forth from the store to the grill to help my mom, Rosie's been working the desk and the store register and Mimi's helping where needed and, of course, 'supervising.'"

"I've got to get busy again myself," Maggie agreed, glad they'd had at least those twenty minutes of respite from the holiday chaos.

The conversation with her cousin stayed with her as she returned to work. It wasn't that she didn't want to be married someday, maybe have a family of her own. But her sister's bad experience with her first marriage had made Maggie wary of making a similar mistake. Hannah had been so sure that she was in love with Wade, that they would be together for a lifetime, that he deserved all the love and loyalty she had offered him. She had been so wrong. Maggie was still amazed that Hannah had found the courage to love again after that fiasco, even though it was obvious to anyone that Andrew Walker was the polar opposite of Wade Cavender.

But Wade had fooled everyone at first, she reminded herself, and Hannah had been very mistaken about her feelings for him. The ugly breakup had been painful, both for Hannah and her family, the repercussions lasting long after the marriage ended.

Fortunately, no children had been involved in that divorce. Garrett McHale came packaged with two vulnerable and impressionable daughters who had already been through a family breakup and the loss of a parent. It would require someone very special to take on the role of stepmother to them—someone confident, tenacious, maybe either trained or at least experienced with adolescent angst. With the girls involved, the stakes were much too high for reckless optimism.

So maybe she had a bit of a crush on Garrett. Maybe the memory of kissing him had taunted her during the night, influenced a few spicy dreams. Maybe parts of her ached to be close to him again, held tightly against that long, lean, muscled body. Maybe she'd like to spend more time with him, to coax out a few more of his sexy smiles, to hear his even sexier low laugh. Maybe she'd like to hike with him, ride horses with him, fly again with him. Maybe there were more things she would like to do with him that she wouldn't allow herself to specify at the moment.

Every time she thought of actually pursuing any of those things beyond a fleeting few hours, she smacked into the reality of his daughters and their fragile sense of security.

She wouldn't let herself be influenced by all the happy newlyweds in her family. She had things to do, places to go before she took that momentous step. Garrett didn't seem to be in any hurry to add more burdens to his already heavy load. So if she could occasionally help him relax and have fun—having a good time herself in the process—without causing any further complications in either of their busy lives, then why not? Her grandmother, and probably his, would be happy to know that there was nothing more to it than that.

Though perhaps it would be necessary for her to remind herself occasionally.

Chapter Six

"I don't think things are going the way we planned with Maggie and Dad," Kix said somberly to her sister Thursday afternoon. They'd had a pretty good day so far with swimming, boating, a nice walk with their dad and Grammy, a good lunch followed by a game of Horse at the basketball court. Payton and their dad hadn't even argued today—much—but now Payton was getting all sulky again because she wanted to go hang out with those boys and she knew their dad would say no if she asked.

Standing at the lakeside behind their cabin, Payton threw a rock into the choppy blue water. It hit the shore in shallow waves kicked up by passing boats and personal watercraft. "It's not my fault Dad's such a nerd."

"Well, no. But maybe he's been so busy worrying about you that he hasn't been able to concentrate on Maggie," Kix said with the wisdom of her newly marked eleven years.

Payton looked resentfully over her shoulder toward the back deck of the cottage. Their dad sat in a wooden patio chair at a round wooden table shaded by a cheery blue-and-white-striped umbrella. His laptop was open on the table in front of him and he appeared to be focused intently on the screen. He was well out of hearing range, but his daughters had no doubt he knew exactly where they were and what they were doing.

"Look at him up there watching us like we're babies who need a full-time sitter," Payton grumbled. "You think he'll go with us to our proms in a few years? Or will he even let us accept an invitation?"

Kix shrugged and knelt to examine a crawfish hole. "It's a long time until either of us goes to prom," she said prosaically.

"If it's up to Dad, we'll never go."

Two teenage boys on personal watercraft passed not far from shore, kicking up rooster tails of water behind them. One of them waved at Payton, who immediately posed to better show off her denim shorts and her cute red T-shirt embellished with an American flag across the chest. She'd selected the outfit specifically to mark the holiday—and, she'd confided artlessly to Kix, because it looked really good on her. She thought Trevor Ferguson kind of liked her, and he was sort of cute even if he had a dorky laugh.

Kix thought maybe her sister was a little too focused on boys, though she had little doubt Trevor was crushing on Payton. After all, Payton was so pretty—just like their mom had been. And she had a way of wearing her hair and clothes that made her look older than she was, unlike Kix, whom everyone mistook for younger.

That was something Payton had in common with Maggie—looking pretty without seeming to put a lot of effort into it. Kix didn't care that much about clothes and hairstyles yet, though she did like the cute purse Maggie had made for her. But she liked it when Maggie talked to her without treating her like a little kid.

It would be nice if their dad and Maggie got together, Kix thought wistfully. As much as she loved her grandmother and great-grandmother, they just didn't always understand what it was like to be young. Maggie was so cool—and she made their dad smile in a different way than he smiled at her and Payton. Maybe if their dad and Maggie got together, Dad would relax his rules a little so she and Payton wouldn't feel like someone was hovering over them all the time. And maybe she wouldn't see that sort of sad look in his eyes sometimes when he didn't know she was looking—the look that always made her wonder if he missed his friends in the air force, or if he was lonely for someone besides his kids and his mother and grandmother. She thought her dad and Maggie made a really cute couple—if only Payton would behave and not scare Maggie away for good.

Though the fireworks would be visible from most any place in the resort, many guests gathered on the grassy compound around the pavilion and playground. Sitting in lawn chairs and on beach towels and blankets spread on the grass, they laughed and chatted as darkness fell over the lake and the grounds. Children ran giggling around their parents, heedless of the sticky warmth of the evening or the occasional buzz of a flying insect.

Maggie's dad and Aaron had set up an old-fashioned popcorn cart in the pavilion, illuminated by strings of red, white and blue lights. The enticing aroma of popping corn wafted through the area. Maggie's mom and aunt Linda handed out free bags to the eager guests who milled around them before claiming viewing spots on the grassy expanse outside the structure. Most had brought their own water, sodas or beer in small coolers. Maggie's dad, her uncle C.J. and Aaron walked casually through the grounds, exchanging greetings with guests but also keeping a close eye on things.

Maggie stood near the pavilion, surrounded by yet more members of her family. Her grandparents sat in comfortably padded folding chairs, reigning over the festivities, as they were the king and queen of Bell Resort. Here for the weekend, Hannah and Andrew sat on a spread blanket with little Claire, who sat on her diapered bottom almost bouncing with excitement at the noise and movement surrounding them. It was getting late for her, and occasionally she rubbed her eyes, but she was too intrigued to sleep.

Not far away, Shelby chattered with her brother, Steven, who had also come home for the holiday weekend. The only member of the family missing was their sister Lori, Maggie thought regretfully. Lori had not been back to Texas since she'd run off with Zach last year. Her parents had flown to California in March to see her, returning a week later rather sad but relieved that she wasn't living in squalor or misery. Looking around the jovial, milling crowd of guests waiting eagerly for the first sign of fireworks over the midnight-blue lake, Maggie realized that she had no envy of Hannah, Steven or Lori. She still enjoyed her job here, had no urge to leave anytime soon. This was home, and she loved it. Which didn't mean she wouldn't want to expand her borders eventually, she reminded herself. It was nice to know she'd kept her options open.

"Maggie, Maggie! Hi. When do the fireworks start? Will you watch them with us? We brought bottles of water in case we get thirsty. Is the popcorn for everyone? It smells so good. I love popcorn."

Maggie smiled down at Kix, who bounced eagerly around her. "Hi, Kix. Yes, the popcorn is free for everyone. Why don't you get a bag?"

"Okay, Daddy?" she asked, checking over her shoulder.

Looking more casual than usual in a T-shirt, khaki cargo shorts and sandals, a folded blanket beneath one arm and a small cooler in his other hand, Garrett smiled slightly and nodded. "Bring a bag for me, too."

She grinned broadly. "I will. Come on, Payton, let's get popcorn."

Payton followed a little more sedately, though she looked just as pleased as Kix by the prospect of the fresh-popped treat.

"Where's the rest of the family?" Maggie asked Garrett as he popped the blanket efficiently onto an unclaimed square of grass.

"Mom and Meemaw are going to watch the show from the back deck. They knew the girls wanted to join everyone here, so they told us to come without them. To be honest, I think they enjoy the quiet occasionally."

Even from several feet away, Maggie could hear Kix chattering to her mom and aunt. She laughed. "Maybe they do."

"Here's your popcorn, Daddy." Scattering kernels behind her like bread crumbs, Kix thrust an overfilled red-and-white-striped bag at him. "Doesn't it smell good? Miss Sarah and Miss Linda said they've got lots more to pop so we can have some more, if we want. When do the fireworks start?"

Garrett looked up at the rapidly darkening sky. "Not much longer."

"They're scheduled to begin at nine," Maggie said. "So we've got almost fifteen more minutes."

Kix sat cross-legged on the blanket with her popcorn and a bottle of water from the cooler. "Oh, I didn't get you any popcorn, Maggie," she said just as she got settled. "Want me to get you some?"

"Thanks, sweetie, but I'm not very hungry. I don't think I could eat a whole bag of popcorn."

Garrett lowered himself to the blanket and patted the space beside him. "You can share mine," he told her with a smile.

Awareness rippled through her. Conscious of his daughters watching them, she sat on the blanket, leaving a respectable amount of space between herself and Garrett. He held out the bag of popcorn and she took a few kernels from the top, her gaze locking with his as she did so.

Like most everyone else around them, Maggie wore shorts and a cool top in patriotic colors in deference to both the holiday and the heat. She pushed a strand of hair away from her face, feeling the stickiness on her skin. There wasn't even a breeze to relieve the warmth that had built up during the day and hadn't yet dissipated with sundown. Sliding off her flip-flops, she sat cross-legged like Kix, though she ruefully admitted to herself that she wasn't quite as comfortable in the position as the girl appeared to be.

"I've been so busy today that I never got a chance to even say hi," she said, addressing the comment to all three McHales. "Have you had a good day?"

Kix, of course, burst into speech before her sister or father had a chance to answer, giving Maggie a detailed play-by-play description of their busy day. Payton was patient for a while, but then claimed some attention for herself. "Do you think my hair would look good shorter, Maggie? Like maybe with bangs or cut in an asymmetrical wedge or something? I think it looks like a kid's cut now."

Maggie reached out to brush a wavy auburn tress from Payton's cheek, thinking that the girl really was going to be stunningly beautiful in a few years. Already the gangliness of childhood was being replaced by a graceful litheness. It was no wonder Garrett was worried about the way boys were starting to look at her.

"I wouldn't do anything drastic," she advised. "Maybe take it just a little shorter and see how you like it first before you make too big a change."

"I keep telling Dad I'm old enough for makeup, but he won't let me wear any," Payton grumbled.

"Oh, goodness, as perfect as your skin is, you don't want to hide it behind makeup," Maggie assured her. "A little lip gloss would be all you need for now, maybe just a touch of mascara for special occasions."

Payton shot a look at her father. He shrugged. "We'll discuss it."

Judging from Payton's pleased expression, that was almost as good as a yes. Kix beamed at Maggie in approval, making her think she'd done something right that time. Why did it always feel to her as if these girls were putting her to some unspoken tests to which she didn't know the rules?

Maybe Payton felt like pushing her luck just a little. "Trevor and Drake are right over there," she said, motioning toward the teens sitting on the grass several yards away and looking over their shoulders at her. Maggie saw the boys' mom and stepdad in lawn chairs closer to the pavilion, talking with another couple who also lounged in folding chairs. "Could I please go watch the fireworks with them, Dad? We'll be right there where you can see us. Kix can even come, if she wants."

"I'd rather stay with Daddy and Mag— Um, yeah, I'll come with you," Kix amended hastily after a look from her sister.

"Please, Dad."

After only a beat during which both girls—and Maggie—held their breath, Garrett nodded. "All right. But don't wander off. And don't get rowdy. Be considerate of the people sitting around you."

Payton's smile was blinding. "We will. Thanks, Dad. Come on, Kix."

Garrett offered the popcorn bag to Maggie as they watched the girls run to join the grinning Ferguson brothers. "Lip gloss, huh?"

His glum tone made her laugh as she took another handful of popcorn. "Just a touch. Face it, Garrett, they're going to grow up no matter how hard you fight it."

"Won't stop me from trying to slow it down a little," he retorted, then tossed a couple of kernels into his mouth and crunched down hard on them.

She looked at his girls laughing and interacting with the Ferguson brothers—Payton flirting, Kix chattering—and she couldn't say she blamed him. "So I take it Payton's not in too much trouble for her stunt yesterday?" she asked after washing down her popcorn with a sip of bottled water.

Garrett shrugged. "I made her apologize to Mom

and promise that she wouldn't run off again without permission, but I didn't see any need to ruin the rest of the week over it."

She nodded in approval and shifted into a more comfortable position on the blanket, her knees drawn up in front of her. "At least Stu's not with them. Maybe his family has moved on."

"I hope so. That kid just wasn't right." He glanced beyond her to where other members of the Bell family mingled. "Looks like your whole clan is here for the holiday weekend."

"All but Lori," she agreed, glancing over her shoulder. "Mimi and Pop are tickled to have everyone here, especially the baby."

She noted that Mimi did not look particularly pleased when their gazes met. Mimi obviously disapproved of Maggie sitting with Esther Lincoln's family rather than her own, even though Esther wasn't there. Mimi would just have to get over that. Maggie didn't choose her friends based on her grandmother's old feuds.

Garrett nodded toward the infant now bouncing in Bryan's arms. "Seems like it was only yesterday my girls were that age."

Maggie smiled at the besotted look on her father's face. Claire had him wrapped firmly around her little fingers, just as she did everyone else who knew and loved her. She then glanced sympathetically at Garrett. "Andrew's already fretting about when Claire notices boys—and she's barely ten months old."

He shook his head as if pushing thoughts of future issues to the back of his mind and asked, "So you had a busy day? Anything exciting happen?"

"Just the usual workday, with the addition of some holiday complications. Nothing too serious."

Before he could answer, a murmur of excitement went through the crowd. The patriotic music blaring from the barge in the lake sounded tinny, but no one seemed to mind as anticipation built for the start of the fireworks show.

"Kix is bouncing again," Maggie said, leaning closer to Garrett so he could hear her over the music and surrounding chatter.

He followed the direction of her gaze and chuckled. "I should have named her Tigger."

"I love how excited she gets about things."

"Me, too," he admitted. "Even though she does wear me out at times."

She bumped his shoulder intentionally with hers as she dug into the offered bag for more popcorn. "Hence my suggestion that you take the occasional me day," she reminded him.

"Still willing to give a few more lessons in me time?" he asked, his eyes more serious than his tone as he looked at her in the glow of the decorative pavilion lights.

"Of course. We're seeing a movie soon, right?"

"Sounds good to me. I just wasn't sure if you'd changed your mind."

Leaning back on her arms on the blanket, she cocked her head to study him. "Why would I do that?"

He started to answer, but was interrupted by the first whooshing pop of a firework being shot into the sky. "Never mind," he said, and leaned back beside her, propping the half-emptied bag of popcorn between them.

The next twenty minutes were filled with colorful explosions, choruses of oohs and aahs, the acrid smell of gunpowder and drifting clouds of smoke. Maggie leaned closer to Garrett so he could hear her comments about her favorite displays of colors and patterns. Late in the show, she gasped in delight when one particularly impressive shell threw glittering gold and silver stars across the black sky. The crowd around them cheered in approval. She turned her head to see if Garrett was as impressed as she, only to find him looking back at her, his mouth curved into a smile that ignited a series of little explosions deep inside her.

The sounds around her faded, all the other people becoming no more than background to the sight of Garrett sprawled casually on the blanket, his blue-gray eyes reflecting the colored lights, his hand resting only an inch or so from her own. His fingers moved, brushed against hers, and she shivered a little even in the July heat.

She'd let down her guard that evening. Forgotten for the past hour to lock up her emotions around him. Her intention had been to appreciate his appeal, to savor the time she had with him, to enjoy his company without getting emotionally involved. Like her other past relationships. But those other men hadn't made her shiver in the heat of a summer night with only a brush of their fingers.

Could be problematic.

"May I walk you home tonight?" Garrett asked, his breath warm against her cheek as he leaned closer to be heard over the noise. "We'll have to go the long way, of course, to drop off the girls at the cabin first."

All things considered, she should probably make an excuse. Yet even as that thought crossed her mind, she heard herself saying, "It's a nice night for a long walk."

Another sexy smile from him made her swallow hard, then look hastily toward the sky again. "Here's the big finale. Should be spectacular."

"I'm sure it will be," she thought she heard him murmur. She didn't quite have the nerve to look at him to see if he was watching the show.

The fireworks show ended to thunderous applause from the audience. It wasn't the largest or most elaborate display most of them had probably seen, but Maggie thought everyone around her looked quite satisfied, which would especially please the older generations of Bells. She offered to help with cleanup afterward, but her dad and Aaron assured her it was all taken care of.

"You're in charge of indoor cleanup," her dad reminded her with a laconic grin. "Outdoors is mine. Go enjoy the rest of your evening. You'll be starting early tomorrow."

She rose on tiptoes to kiss his sun-weathered cheek. "Happy Fourth, Dad."

He patted her arm with a callused hand. "You, too, hon."

She turned to find Garrett again, her gaze meeting Shelby's as she did so. The knowing look on Shelby's face made Maggie wrinkle her nose as she remembered their conversation from earlier. Nothing had changed, she reminded herself. She had her defenses firmly back in place now. Shelby could tease all she wanted later, but Maggie wouldn't let it get to her.

"Ready?" Garrett asked when she stepped up beside him.

She tossed back her hair and lifted her chin. "I'm ready."

One of his eyebrows rose a bit in response to something he must have heard in her voice, but he merely stepped back and motioned in the direction of his daughters. She moved toward them, aware of him following closely behind her, carrying the cooler and the neatly refolded blanket.

"Let's go, girls. Time to head back to the cabin," he said, giving the boys a nod. Maggie thought he must have made an effort to sound congenial, probably for Payton's sake, but the boys still looked a little intimidated by him, she noted in amusement.

Payton just never seemed to know when to quit when she was ahead. "Trevor said he and Drake will walk me back later," she said airily. "They'll make sure I get back okay. I won't be much longer."

Garrett sighed and gave Maggie a look of exasperation. She had to admit he'd tried to end the evening pleasantly. This one was on Payton. "You'll come now," he said. "Maggie's going to walk with us. Tell your friends good-night."

"Dad—"

"C'mon, Payton," Kix said with a groan. "Can't you just let it go for once?"

"We'll see you tomorrow, Payton," Trevor said, moving quickly backward. "If your dad lets you, of course."

Maggie wasn't sure if that was merely a comment or another little dig about Garrett's close supervision, but Payton flushed, obviously taking it as the latter. She turned with a huff and headed in the direction of the cabin.

Kix skipped along at Maggie's side. The gunpowder smell still hung in the warm air and streams of resort guests moved toward the motel, cabins and campgrounds, while others who'd come just for the day's festivities piled into cars to leave the grounds. Even the cacophony of conversation, laughter and car engines seemed rather quiet compared to the noise of the fireworks. An occasional bang and eruption of twinkling color came from other parts of the lake, but private fireworks were banned within the resort. Stars had appeared overhead, dimmed by the yellowish security lighting but still visible, as was the sliver of the last-quarter moon.

"Weren't the fireworks beautiful, Maggie? Which ones did you like best? I liked the red ones that filled up the whole sky. Or maybe those silver ones that whistled and shot around all over the place like they were in a big pinball machine or something. Payton likes the blue ones, don't you, Payton? Which ones did you like, Maggie?"

Maggie rested a hand lightly on Kix's shoulder. "I like all of them. Every time I think I see my favorite, the next one is even better."

"Me, too. They were all so pretty. Are you coming in with us when we get to the cabin?"

"No, your dad offered to walk me home after we drop off you and Payton."

"Oh, that was nice of him," Kix said artlessly. "That way you won't have to walk by yourself. Wasn't that nice, Payton?"

Payton sniffed. "At least *her* dad didn't say she couldn't walk with whoever she wanted."

"We are not having this conversation again, Payton," Garrett snapped. "You can pout all you want, but I decide what rules are appropriate for a thirteen-year-old."

Kix hurried to Payton's side and whispered something rather urgently. Maggie figured the younger girl was asking her sister not to ruin the nice evening. Whatever words she'd used, they seemed to have an effect. Payton hesitated, then nodded grumpily. "Okay. Sorry, Maggie. I didn't mean to sound so grumpy. And, uh, sorry, Dad."

He sounded just a little surprised when he replied, "Yeah, okay."

He and Maggie exchanged quizzical looks. She smiled and shrugged slightly. Just because she'd once been a thirteen-year-old girl didn't mean she fully understood their thought processes now.

"It's getting late," Garrett said to the girls when they reached the cabin. "You should go ahead and take your baths and get ready for bed. Tomorrow is another busy day."

"You don't have to hurry back, Daddy," Kix assured him. "We'll get ourselves to bed. If you and Maggie want to have coffee or something, that's okay."

Payton cleared her throat loudly, giving her sister a look Maggie couldn't interpret.

"Just go to bed and let Maggie and me decide whether we want coffee," Garrett growled with a shake of his head.

Kix gave him a big hug. "Good night, Daddy."

Maggie watched as he leaned down to kiss his younger daughter's cheek. "Good night, sweetheart."

Payton stepped up to lean briefly against him. "'Night, Dad. Don't forget to tell Maggie what a nice guy uncle Jay is."

After a pause on her father's part, as if he was trying to decide what she meant by that, Payton, too, got a kiss on the cheek.

Kix almost tackled Maggie with a hug then. Laughing, Maggie embraced her in return, dropping a light kiss on the girl's disheveled hair. Her parting with Payton was somewhat more restrained, but just as affectionate.

She and Garrett watched as the girls ran inside the cabin to join their grandmother and great-grandmother.

Only then did she turn to Garrett. "What on earth was that about you telling me about what a nice guy Jay is?"

Pushing a hand through his short hair, Garrett gave a short grunt. "Beats the hell out of me. Sometimes I think my kids make an effort to keep me confused."

Chuckling, she wrapped a hand around his arm. "Poor Garrett. You really are overwhelmed by the women in your family, aren't you?"

"You can say that again." Matching their steps, they began to move toward the family compound and her mobile home.

The day's heat had eased now, leaving the air still warm but more comfortable. Settling down for the night, guests sat around low-banked campfires, talking and laughing, the drone of voices carrying through the night without intelligible words. The resort's official quiet hours began at ten, so anyone being too loud or disruptive would be asked to tone it down. With the exception of the occasional drunken disturbance, there was rarely cause for any official action on the part of her family in their role as owners and managers.

She and Garrett cut across the road through the tent campgrounds. He slid his hand down her arm to lace his fingers with hers, seemingly with all the time in the world just to walk her home. "This is more my type of camping," he commented, nodding toward a small group gathered around a campfire with a simple lantern lighting the pad on which their tents rested. "The fancy RVs are nice, but I always kind of liked sleeping in a bag on a canvas tent floor with a rock digging into my butt."

"Sounds like a military man."

"Guess that explains it. My family, now, they either want a nice cabin or one of those fancy RVs. With bathrooms, showers and electrical outlets, and preferably a TV and a microwave."

"I would think the girls would enjoy tent camping."

He shrugged. "They did when they were younger. I took them hiking and camping a few times on my custody weekends. Kix might still enjoy it, but Payton wants the luxuries now."

"A phase," she assured him. "She probably still likes hiking and camping, she just doesn't want to risk being uncool by admitting it."

He groaned. "I'm doing my best to teach her not to measure her self-worth by what other people think of her. To be herself without giving a damn whether others think she's cool. I wish she wasn't so concerned about her image these days."

"It's so much a part of being a teenager. But I think it's vital that you continue to reassure her it's important to be herself. I had that sort of grounding from my parents, and it made a difference in keeping me out of what we call 'the game.'"

"The game?"

She nodded. "The one where you try to have newer cars or more expensive clothes or shoes or flashier electronics or bigger houses than everyone else. My dad told us repeatedly that it's a game you can never win because there's always someone prettier, richer, flashier, more popular just waiting in the wings. He said we could destroy our health and happiness and ruin our credit and empty our bank accounts trying to get ahead, but the only way to be truly happy and content is not to play in the first place. He said we should follow our own bliss and count our blessings.

"Obviously he hoped our bliss would keep us here at the resort with the family," she added, "but my parents didn't try to stop Hannah from making a home in Dallas and they wouldn't interfere if I suddenly announced that I want to spend a year in Europe or some other wild dream."

"You want to spend a year in Europe?"

She laughed and shook her head. "No. It was an example."

"Ah."

"You're a good dad, Garrett."

He kept his eyes on the road ahead. "I try."

"I know."

Reaching the end of the road through the tent-camping area, they crossed the main road to reach the drive to the family compound. On the other side of the Private Drive sign, pools of yellow light illuminated the asphalt road from overhead security lamps. The lamps were fairly new, having been installed last summer after Shelby was kidnapped in deep shadows while walking this same road alone late at night. Growing up in the resort, they'd had no concerns about walking anywhere at any hour, but her ordeal had given the family reason to initiate a few new precautions. They refused still to live in fear, but because Andrew was in the security and investigation business, they now followed his advice on some basic safety practices.

She had no concerns about walking in the dark with her current companion—not physically, anyway. Her only vulnerability where Garrett was involved was letting herself forget that she wanted to keep any developments between them relaxed and superficial. When it came to this intriguing man, she was definitely conflicted. As much as she wanted to be with him, as deeply as she craved to touch and be touched by him, she was still convinced that any affair between them—

if that was where this led—had to stay casual. Private. Thinking of his daughters again, she frowned. "Seriously, Garrett, what did Kix mean when she told you to tell me about Jay? Why would that occur to her just then?"

He made a sound that was a cross between a sigh and a grumble. For a moment, she thought that was the only reply she was going to get, but then he said reluctantly, "I think the girls may be considering a fix-up."

"Between Jay and me?" she asked with a raised eyebrow.

"They might have mentioned something about it."

She laughed softly. "Not going to happen."

"That's what I told them. Wait, why did *you* reject it so fast? You like Jay, don't you?"

"I like him very much. But me and a preacher? No way."

He half turned to look at her as they walked. "Philosophical objection?"

"No. After all, I choose to attend his services almost every week and I enjoy them. It's just too much responsibility for me. All those members of his congregation and their expectations. All the duties inherent in being a pastor's wife. You know how I feel about being free to do my own thing—Jay doesn't have that advantage."

"I see." Garrett left it at that.

Deciding to change the subject, she motioned toward the row of three redbrick ranch-style houses on her left. "That's my uncle C.J. and aunt Sarah's house. The one in the center is the original, the one my grandparents live in. On the right is the house where my sister and I grew up."

"Nice. One big backyard."

"The whole resort was our backyard," she said. She

pointed ahead. "There are the trailers my generation moved into, much to Pop's disapproval. Steven and Shelby own the ones on the left, while mine and Hannah's are on the right. Mine's the last one on the right."

Just beyond the trailers, the road dead-ended in a cul-de-sac. Lights burned in all the trailers, but no one was outside, giving them a semblance of privacy as they approached her front door. Something moved in the shadows, and a large, aging yellow Lab ambled up to them. Maggie rested a hand on the broad, flat head. "This is Pax. Officially, he's Steven's dog, but we all take care of him now that Steven's away most of the time. He's sort of the family mascot."

"Hey, Pax." Garrett offered a hand for the dog to sniff, then rubbed his floppy ears. "How's it going?"

The dog grinned and lazily wagged his tail, enjoying the ear massage.

Maggie pulled her keys out of her pocket. "Would you like to come in for that coffee Kix offered?" she asked lightly. "I can make decaf. Or tea, if you prefer."

"I'm not sure if I should."

She tilted her head to look up at him. "Why not?"

After glancing around the compound, he tugged her against him in the shadow of her home. "This is why," he murmured, and pressed his mouth to hers.

She melted into him, her arms going around his neck, her lips parting eagerly for him. She could tell him—and herself—as often as she wanted that they could keep this casual, but that didn't change the fact that all he had to do was touch her and her entire body went on high alert. As closely as he held her, it was very obvious that she wasn't the only one to react that way, which didn't make it any easier to resist him.

Drawing her mouth from his, she looked up at him.

His face was heavily shadowed, but she could make out the feverish glitter in his eyes, the tense line of his cheek and jaw. She brought a hand around to his face and felt the jump of muscle beneath her fingertips. "You don't have to hurry back to the cabin, do you? Why don't you come in?"

"You're sure?"

Stepping back, she took his hand. "Let's just go inside, Garrett."

He made no further effort to resist.

Chapter Seven

She had decorated her mobile home in sage and cream—soothing colors chosen for quiet relaxation. Yet she wasn't at all relaxed when she led Garrett into her home. Every nerve ending still buzzed with awareness of him. He closed the door behind him with a solid click that she echoed with a hard swallow. She felt her fingers tremble—not with apprehension, but with anticipation. Despite her determination not to let things get out of hand with Garrett, not to complicate either his life or her own, they could have this, she assured herself. A little private time to enjoy each other, to savor their mutual attraction, to explore the chemistry between them. It didn't have to lead to anything awkward or binding, might never happen again, for that matter, but they had tonight. It would be a shame if they wasted this rare, fleeting opportunity.

She'd left a lamp burning, and she didn't bother to

turn on any more lights. Garrett put a hand to the back of his neck and squeezed, looking a little uncertain. It really had been a while since he'd done anything like this, she thought with a slight smile. For some reason, she found herself gaining confidence in response to his hesitance.

"You look like a man who could use a good rub-down," she said gravely, moving toward him. "I bet those poor neck and shoulder muscles are tied in knots."

He dropped his hand, looking suddenly self-conscious. "Payton tends to do that to me," he admitted, his tone wry. "It's her special talent."

She didn't want to talk about his kids just now. Didn't want him to think about anything or anyone outside these walls. Even if only for this one time.

Standing close in front of him, she slid a hand up his arm to his shoulder. "Just for tonight, let me be the one to undo it. I give a mean massage."

"I'll just bet you do."

She tugged lightly at the sleeve of his T-shirt. "I could get to those knots more easily if this was out of the way."

In one smooth move, he grabbed the hem of his shirt and tugged upward, then tossed the shirt over the arm of a chair. The lamplight gleamed on his tanned skin, revealing the ridges of muscle and ribs and a scatter-ing of dark hair that narrowed intriguingly down to the waistband of his shorts. A few interesting scars were visible, but didn't detract from his appeal—just the op-posite, in fact, as they added to the overall impression of virile masculinity. She would love to hear the story be-hind each one—but not now, she decided, pressing her palms to his chest to savor the heat and strength of him.

He rested his hands on her hips, and the hint of a

tremor gave her a clue to the willpower it took for him to keep the contact light. "Where would you like to perform this miracle massage?" he asked, his voice a little huskier than usual.

Trailing one fingertip down the center of his torso to his waistband, she smiled when his stomach contracted sharply beneath her touch. "Well, it would be difficult for me to reach all the spots with you towering over me like this. You should probably sit down. Or better yet, lie down."

"Wherever you want me."

She liked the sound of that. "This way," she said, and turned toward her bedroom.

A few minutes later, he lay facedown on her bed, his face turned to one side, hands laced beneath his cheek. She straddled him, legs gripping his slender hips as she took her time working out the kinks. Again, she'd turned on only one lamp, and that on low, so that deep shadows surrounded the bed, leaving them cocooned in a soft pool of light. Just the two of them.

His skin was warm and supple beneath her hands. She loved the feel of it, admiring the solid foundation of muscle beneath. All that running he'd mentioned certainly paid off for him.

Garrett gave a low groan, part pain, mostly pleasure, when she attacked one particularly stubborn knot at the base of his neck. "Another knot to attribute to Payton?" she asked with a faint chuckle.

"Actually, I think that one has your name on it."

Her hands stilled in surprise. "Mine?"

Suddenly shifting his weight, he rolled to his back, reaching up to hold her in place on top of him. She steadied herself by flattening her palms against his chest, her gaze locking with his glittering blue-gray eyes. The hard ridge beneath his shorts clued her in that he wasn't nearly as relaxed as he'd seemed only moments earlier.

He wasn't the only one tied in knots now. She felt the tension building low in her abdomen, spreading through her limbs. The atmosphere in the room changed from soothing and comfortable to almost sparking with heightened awareness.

Garrett reached up to cup her face in his hands. "Definitely yours," he said and brought her mouth down to his own.

"Then I should probably do something about that," she murmured against his lips.

Moving again, he twisted to flip her beneath him. She landed on her back against the pillows, breathless, laughing, tingling with anticipation. "Or maybe we can both work on that one," she said.

He nibbled at her jaw, his hand sliding down her body. "I'm thinking I should return the favor. Got any places that need my personal attention?"

He had already found one such place. His hand had slipped between them to find her breast, cupping and kneading until her breathing quickened. She arched instinctively into his touch, her voice shaky when she murmured, "I'm sure I'll think of a few."

His grin slashed white in the dim lighting. "Happy to be of service."

Chuckling softly, she tugged his head downward, bringing his mouth to hers even as his hands began a thorough search for all those spots that craved his attention.

Propped on one arm, Garrett used his free hand to brush a damp strand of hair from Maggie's cheek, tucking it behind her ear. She lay on her back beside him, a sheet draped over her to the tops of her bare breasts, her breathing still slightly accelerated but gradually slowing. Her arms and legs felt heavy, but deliciously so. She didn't know about him, but she didn't have a tense knot left in her body. Judging by the relaxed lines of his face and mouth, he felt much the same way.

He sighed, as much with reluctance as satisfaction. "I should go. It's getting late."

Her sigh echoed his. "I suppose you should."

"Thanks for the, um, massage. I'm feeling a lot better now."

She laughed softly. "You're welcome. Maybe we'll do it again sometime."

Gazing down at her, he murmured, "I'd like that."

"So would I," she said, assuring herself that they were keeping the tone light and casual, just the way it should be. No promises, no commitments. No reason at all to fear that she had just made a huge mistake that had the power to hurt not only her but too many innocent bystanders, as well.

She swallowed hard.

Unaware of the uncomfortable direction her thoughts had taken, Garrett gave her a lingering kiss, then rolled to reach for his clothes. Shaking her head to clear her conflicted thoughts, Maggie slipped into the soft terry robe she kept near her bed to walk him out. Garrett dressed quickly, running a hand through his short hair to straighten it. By the time they stood by her door, the only evidence of their recent activity was his notably relaxed smile.

"Don't forget about the open-air concert tomorrow night at the pavilion," she reminded him. "The girls will probably enjoy it."

The mention of his daughters just then was deliberate. A reminder to both of them that real life waited just outside her door, and that everything was different out there.

He groaned. "Payton will probably want to slow-dance with the Ferguson brothers."

"We're not setting up a dance floor," she assured him with a chuckle. "Just bring your blanket to sit on again. Maybe a picnic dinner would be fun for the girls."

"I'll ask them."

"And, Garrett?" Since they'd brought up the topic of his kids, she might as well make the suggestion she'd been meaning to share with him. "Maybe it would help if you let Payton spend a little time with the Ferguson brothers? With you in the nearby vicinity, of course— maybe at the pool or the swim beach or the basketball court."

He started to frown, and she hastened to explain her reasoning. "I'm thinking right now the boys seem like intriguing forbidden fruit to her. They've probably been on their best behavior with her, flirting and flattering and feigning maturity. But maybe if she spends a little more time with them, they'll start acting like themselves—in other words, normal, goofy adolescent boys—and some of the illusion will wear thin."

"Or she could be more influenced by them and become even more rebellious than she already has been."

Maggie shrugged ruefully, thinking of her cousin Lori, who'd fallen hard for a young man with a troubled past of whom her family had vehemently disapproved. They had all but forbidden her to see him—which she had resented to the point that she'd eloped with him, to her parents' shock and dismay. But Payton was thirteen, not twenty, and neither of the young Ferguson brothers was a brooding aspiring rock star like Lori had fallen for. "That's always a possibility, I suppose. But more likely, she'll see Trevor and Drake acting like clowns or squabbling like regular siblings and some of their appeal will wear off. Whereas you, on the other hand, will look a bit more like a cool dad."

His frown had been replaced by a very faint, wry smile. "And less like an unreasonable tyrant?"

She shrugged. "Maybe. I'm no expert in raising kids, of course, but I'm trying to remember what it was like to be thirteen."

"You were at that stage a lot more recently than I was," he conceded with a slight wince.

Did the age difference between them bother him? She hadn't given it that much thought. "You're hardly a senior citizen," she teased him.

"Still closer than you are."

She crossed her hands behind his neck to grin up at him. "I like my men like my wine—aged enough to make them interesting."

Chuckling, he bent his head to brush a kiss across her lips. "Is that right?"

"Absolutely. Much more intoxicating that way," she assured him with a laugh that was cut off when he kissed her more thoroughly.

He left after a few more heated minutes, stepping away from her with a show of unenthusiastic determination. "Okay, I'm leaving. Good night, Maggie. I'll see you around tomorrow."

She locked the door behind him, then turned back toward the bedroom. As much as she told herself that this was all very easy and casual and string-free, she still suspected that it would be a while before she got to sleep that night. She feared she was going to over-

think this no matter how much she resisted doing so—
not her usual style, but then, nothing about her feelings
for Garrett was quite like anything she'd felt before.

Garrett was rather relieved that he didn't encounter
any of Maggie's family on his way back to the cabin.
The lights were on in most of the family homes, but no
one was outside and if anyone peeked out a window to
spot him walking past, they did so without him seeing.
He supposed he shouldn't be particularly concerned.
Maggie had made no effort to conceal his visit from
her family. Living as closely as they all did, it must
be an unwritten rule that personal privacy had to be
respected. And she was, after all, an adult with every
right to entertain whomever she wanted in her home.

She'd kept protection in her nightstand, and had
matter-of-factly produced it at the proper moment.
Still, he would bet his life savings that she was quite
discriminating about whom she invited into her bed.
Which made it even more gratifying that she'd chosen
to be with him tonight, though she continued to make
it clear that she wasn't looking for anything serious to
develop with him. Exactly the way he wanted it, right?

Most of the tent campers seemed to have bedded
down for the night. Red embers gleamed in fire pits, and
folding chairs sat abandoned until morning. He heard
a baby fussing somewhere and a small dog yapped a
time or two, but other than that, the grounds were fairly
quiet, a notable contrast to the noisy celebration earlier. He glanced upward, seeing the blinking lights of
high-flying jets among the scattering of stars. It wasn't
hard for him to mentally place himself in the cockpit, a
complex instrument panel in front of him, black sky all
around him, stars above and city lights below.

He'd thought about flying commercially after retiring from the service. He'd probably have enjoyed it, and still would have had plenty of time for his girls. Of course, that was before Breanne died. Now he couldn't imagine being away from his kids as much as he'd been before, seeing them only on weekends and holidays, or saying goodbye after his court-scheduled visitations. He deeply regretted, of course, that they'd lost their mother, that Breanne had died so young, with so much of her and their daughters' lives ahead of her, but he did not regret making the decision to put them first in his life now, to rearrange all his plans and goals on their behalf. Even when Payton acted out—and he suspected that was going to get worse before he attended her high school graduation—he still wouldn't make any other choice.

He'd given little thought to remarrying, though others had asked him on occasion if he'd considered the possibility. But if he ever did contemplate doing so, it could only be with a woman who loved his girls, who understood his total commitment to them, who wasn't averse to the vast responsibility that came with them. Which meant, all in all, that he'd probably stay single for a while yet. He was good with that.

The light was out in the upstairs window when he approached cabin six, so he figured the girls were asleep. Except for a light in the living room window, the rest of the cabin was also dark. His mom had probably left a lamp burning for him when she and her mother had turned in. At almost midnight, he didn't expect to find anyone awake.

Entering the front door, he paused when he saw his grandmother sitting in her chair, knitting needles clicking rhythmically in the quiet, deeply shadowed living room. The lamp on the table at her side was the only light burning, so she sat in a pool of illumination. Her gleaming white hair gave her an almost angelic appearance—deceptively angelic, Garrett thought with wry amusement.

"Couldn't sleep, Meemaw?"

She shook her head. "Wasn't sleepy yet. You been with that Bell girl?"

His shrug was as close as she was going to get to an answer.

His grandmother studied him over the tops of her glasses. "Wonder what her family thinks about you being over at her place at this hour?"

"I would imagine they think she's an adult who can make her own decisions."

"Hmm. We'll see if you think that way about Payton when she's that age."

Garrett had a fleeting image of Bryan Bell glaring at him the way he'd been eyeing the Ferguson boys. What would Bryan think of his daughter having a no-strings fling with a decade-older divorcé with two kids?

He cleared his throat. "You should get some sleep, Meemaw. Another long day tomorrow."

"I will shortly. So, you see anything long-term developing between you and that girl? Think she's the right one to bring home to your daughters?"

"Neither Maggie nor I is interested in long-term, Meemaw. We just enjoy spending time together occasionally. Don't try to make it into more than that."

His grandmother harrumphed. "Fine with me. It's not like I want Dixie Bell having claim to my great-granddaughters. You just mind that you don't get in over your head with this one. I'd hate to see your heart get broken again. Not to mention the girls' hearts if they get attached to her and then it doesn't work out."

"Breanne didn't break my heart," he protested automatically—and mostly honestly. "Our breakup was mutual."

"It wasn't the woman you grieved for. It was the future you'd envisioned with her. Wouldn't want you to get caught up in that sort of unrealistic fantasy again with the wrong woman."

Because she was eerily echoing his own earlier thoughts, Garrett didn't quite know how to respond. He knew his grandmother meant well in offering advice, but she wasn't exactly a fan of anyone in the Bell family. Nor did she understand that Maggie wasn't angling for him—or anyone else, as far as he could determine. "I'm turning in, Meemaw. You need anything?"

She turned her attention back to her knitting. "I'll be going to bed myself shortly. I'll get the light. See you tomorrow, Garrett."

He nodded and headed for his room, his steps suddenly weary.

Maggie was out early Friday morning. She'd slept only fitfully, though she assured herself she was not obsessing about her deepening feelings for Garrett. She lied, of course, but that made it somewhat easier to get through the night. She was up before dawn, out of her house less than half an hour later. She'd taken a quick shower, left her hair damp and loose, applied a minimum of makeup and dressed in a loose peasant-style top and khaki capris with her favored wedge sandals. Casual, easy and it didn't look as though she'd overthought her appearance for any reason. Just the statement she was trying to make.

Too restless to take a golf cart, she walked briskly toward the main building, intending to get a head start on her workday. There were plenty of early risers among the campers, as evidenced by the faint aromas of coffee and bacon wafting through the crisp early morning air. Boat motors droned on the lake as fishermen headed out to battle the sunrise-feeding fish. It was going to be a blistering hot day, but for now it was just comfortably warm.

The smell of coffee was strong in the main building, too. Her aunt was already bustling around the diner and she knew her uncle had the big pot brewing in the marina. Workdays started early in the resort, especially during peak season. She thought of going into the diner, but she wasn't quite hungry yet. She decided instead to run upstairs to do a little paperwork first. She'd come down for coffee and a bagel with the family afterward. She could usually find two or three of them gathered in the diner for breakfast before the days turned too hectic.

She wasn't expecting to find her grandfather rustling around in Shelby's big desk upstairs. He rarely came up to the office floor these days, and never bothered Shelby's files and ledgers. "Pop? Can I help you find something?"

"Stamps," he grumbled, rummaging in Shelby's pencil drawer in a way that had to be making a terrible mess in there. "Doesn't anyone use stamps anymore? Does everything have to be sent by computer these days? I want to send a birthday card to an old friend and I don't want to have to drive all the way to town for a stamp or send one of those electronic cards through a computer. Wouldn't know how to do that, anyway."

"You won't have to send an e-card, Pop." She nudged him gently out of the way and opened the top right drawer in Shelby's desk. "Here's where she keeps the stamps."

He accepted the stamp with a short nod of gratitude. "You're in early this morning."

"Thought I'd get an early start before it gets too hot."

"That right? I thought maybe you were clearing part of the day to spend time with your new boyfriend's family. Nice family, cute kids. You look good with them."

"He's not my boyfriend, Pop."

"Oh, that's right. You're just 'friends.'" The quotes were most definitely implied in his teasing remark.

She sighed.

Her grandfather patted her cheek. "Maybe I know you a little better than you think, Magpie. I've been watching you with that man. You don't look at him quite the same way you do your other friends."

Maggie decided humor was the best way to handle this discomfiting exchange. "Surely you're not trying to fix me up with Esther Lincoln's grandson, Pop. Whatever would Mimi say about that?"

He chuckled. "I'll tell you a secret about Dixie and Esther. They're quite happy being mortal enemies. Either one of them would miss the other if she wasn't around any longer."

Laughing softly, she nodded. "I've pretty much figured that out. Now I've got a few things to do before I go downstairs for breakfast."

"Just headed down that way myself. Want me to put in an order for you?"

"No, thanks. I'm not sure when I'll get down. You go ahead, though."

He winked at her. "We'll wait on you like one pig waits on another."

She'd been hearing him say that from the day she

was born, but she laughed obligingly anyway. "I'll be down later."

She threw herself into her work as soon as she was alone again, completing paperwork in the office, then responding to a minor emergency call from the staff at the motel to deal with a broken window blind. Normally such issues were passed on to her dad or Aaron or one of the part-time maintenance workers, but because everyone was busy getting the grounds ready for the evening's scheduled activities, she decided to check on it herself first. Fortunately, she was able to make the repair on her own, at least temporarily until a new blind could be ordered, something she would take care of that very afternoon. She never did get around to having breakfast and she stayed too busy to think about… well, anything in particular. Not that she was trying *not* to think, she assured herself at one point. She was simply busy. Very, very busy.

She was walking from cabin three to the main building with her tablet in her hand early that afternoon when she heard her name called. She glanced up from the onscreen checklist to find Payton waving to her from the tennis court. Dressed in shorts and a T-shirt, her auburn hair caught up in a perky ponytail, she swung a tennis racket from her free hand. Her face gleamed with a sheen of perspiration and her smile was almost blindingly bright.

Maggie glanced automatically around for other members of the girl's family—one in particular—but saw only the older Ferguson boy, Trevor, on the other side of the tennis net, bouncing and catching a yellow ball while holding a racket in his other hand. "Hi, Payton. Hello, Trevor," she called out, walking a few steps in their direction.

"Hi, Maggie." Payton had to raise her voice to be heard over the sounds of hammering coming from the rented temporary stage being erected on the grass near the courts.

"Having a good time?" Maggie asked, though the answer was obvious in Payton's smile.

The girl nodded eagerly, making her ponytail swing. "Trevor plays on a tennis team at his school. When I told him I've taken lessons at the country club, we decided to play singles. He's really good, but he's not beating me too bad."

"Payton's good, too," Trevor insisted quickly. "She almost won the last set."

Payton blushed with pleasure and gave him a little shove, the adolescent equivalent of a thank-you.

"Where are the rest of your families?" Maggie asked casually.

"My mom and stepdad took Drake out fishing," Trevor replied. "I didn't want to go. It's too hot to fish in the middle of the day. They're not going to catch anything, but they don't listen to me."

"Dad had to take Meemaw to the pharmacy because she forgot one of her prescriptions needed to be refilled," Payton said. "Kix went with them. Grammy's at the cabin watching her daytime TV. Dad said I could play tennis with Trevor if we stay out of the way of the stage construction and don't go wandering off. We wanted to go swimming but he wouldn't let us do that," she added with a frown. "Not without him there to watch, though he knows I can swim just fine."

"Me, too," Trevor piped up. "I'm on a swim team."

So Garrett had finally loosened up enough to allow Payton a couple hours of unsupervised time with her new friend. Maggie could only imagine with a smoth-

ered smile the list of conditions he'd recited before-
hand. She had to agree with him about the swimming,
though. No lifeguards were provided at the resort, so
she didn't think Garrett was out of line to ask Payton
not to swim without supervision. Not that she intended
to tell Payton that, of course.

"Well, have a good time," she said. "Don't get too hot
out here in the sun. When you've finished your game,
stop by the diner for a cold soda on me, if you like. I'll
tell my aunt to take care of you."

Both teens grinned at her. "Thank you, Maggie."

"You're welcome, Payton. See you later?"

"Sure. Bye." Payton and her friend returned to their
positions on the court.

It was nice to see Payton looking so cheerful for a
change. She was in big-time flip-the-ponytail-and-flirt
mode, which Garrett would hate, but Maggie thought it
was cute. For now. Maybe now that Garrett had loosened his rules to give Payton a little more breathing
space, some of the tension between them would ease,
as well. For both their sakes, she hoped so.

Her stomach growled, and she realized she'd had
nothing all day but a couple of cups of coffee. She an-
gled toward the diner, figuring it wouldn't take long
to eat since it was past the lunchtime rush. Her aunt
greeted her and quickly served her a bowl of chicken-
and-rice soup with crackers. While she was eating, her
grandmother came in and sat beside her.

"Hannah and Andrew brought the baby to my house
for a while," Mimi said with a smile. "That little girl is
cute as a bug's ear. Full of pepper, too. Once she starts
walking, she's going to have her parents hopping to
keep up with her."

Maggie swallowed a spoonful of soup. "I'm sure you're right."

"It's about time for you and Shelby to start thinking about kids of your own," her grandmother pronounced. "Whatever happened to that nice Kennedy boy you dated for a while? I could tell he was crazy about you."

"He married Lisa Porterfield."

"Oh." There was nothing Mimi hated worse than admitting she was wrong about anything—so she rarely did. "Well, I suppose he settled for someone else when you didn't give him any encouragement."

Thinking of how besotted her old friend Brett Kennedy was over Lisa Porterfield, Maggie merely smiled and took another bite of her soup. "This soup is really good, as always, Aunt Sarah."

"Thanks, hon. Your grandmother taught me how to make this recipe not long after your uncle C.J. and I were married. I've never found a better recipe for chicken-and-rice soup."

Mimi nodded in satisfaction, though a slight frown creased her white eyebrows. "I entered this soup in the county extension homemakers' club contest back in '58. It should have won the soup division blue ribbon, but *someone* beat me with the most bland cream of mushroom soup you ever tasted. Might as well have come out of a red-and-white tin can."

Maggie gave a little sigh. It wasn't hard to guess who matched Mimi's hissed "someone."

"I always believed Esther Lincoln made some sort of deal with the judges," her grandmother added in a grumble, verifying Maggie's suspicion. "I find it hard to believe they really liked her soup more than mine. But my cinnamon coffee cake—now, there was no way they couldn't award me the prize for that. Got the blue ribbon for baked goods that year and tied with you-know-who for best of show. She pouted because she thought her fresh strawberry cake should have won the baked goods division, which would have given her full best-of-show title, but not even her friendship with the judges could accomplish that."

Maggie had been hearing this story—and variations on it—all her life, so she merely murmured sympathetically and continued enjoying the second-place-winning soup.

"What about Jason O'Hara?" Mimi asked suddenly. "He and his wife broke up last year, didn't they? Nice enough looking guy and he's doing well with that insurance business. Of course, his sister Janine is a holy terror, with all those public tantrums she throws when things don't go her way, but maybe you wouldn't have to deal with her all that much...."

Maggie shared a wry look with her aunt, but let her grandmother's blatant matchmaking roll off her without remark. It had been going on since Shelby's wedding, and it would likely continue for some time yet. Not to mention that Mimi couldn't disapprove more of Maggie's friendship with Garrett. There was no reason to get defensive, as Hannah or Shelby or especially Lori might have done. Maggie had always been the one to let the little things go for the sake of peace, choosing her rare battles very carefully. Unlike Payton, Maggie had never openly rebelled, quietly following her own path—which, she admitted, had coincided quite a lot with her family's hopes for her. And by causing few problems, she had been more likely to be granted permission for the things she really wanted.

Maybe she could give Payton a few hints about

choosing battles, she mused while her grandmother droned on beside her about local gossip and past indignities. She didn't want to butt in unasked, but maybe she would find a way to gently advise the girl, just as a friend. Garrett seemed to have taken her advice to ease up a bit and that appeared to be working out well enough. Friends helped each other without worrying about getting too deeply involved in each other's lives, right? Just because she wasn't ready for the everyday commitment of parenthood didn't mean she couldn't lend a helping hand occasionally.

Finishing her lunch, she wiped her mouth with her napkin and stood. "I've got a ton of stuff to do before the concert tonight, Mimi. I'll see you later, okay?"

"Don't know what Hannah was thinking scheduling a concert here tonight," her grandmother grumbled. "More likely to bring in a bunch of hooligans than paying customers."

"They have to pay to get in unless they're staying with us," Maggie reminded her indulgently. The entry fee was nominal, but it did discourage some of the troublemakers. "Besides, not many hooligans are interested in the family-friendly concert Hannah put together. A local country band and a couple of folk singers don't usually draw the hard-rock crowd."

She kissed her grandmother's soft cheek, thanked her aunt again, then headed for the exit, nodding to guests as she passed them. She really did have a lot to do before the concert. Her chores would keep her much too busy to worry about Garrett and Payton's relationship— or to endlessly replay every moment of her lovemaking with Garrett. She would save that for later, when she was alone in her bed and very likely wishing he were there with her again.

* * *

"So your dad is chilling out some, huh?"

In response to Trevor's question, Payton glanced over her shoulder some distance away to where her father sat talking with Maggie, who sat on the blanket beside him, her knees drawn up in front of her, arms draped loosely around them. Each seemed more interested in the other than in the twangy country music being played by the band on the temporary stage. Seeing the look on her dad's face, Payton felt a funny feeling somewhere deep inside her stomach. Had she ever seen him look at anyone else quite like that? She didn't think so.

Totally uninterested in the concert, Payton, Kix and the Ferguson brothers were at the playground along with quite a few younger kids. Payton and Trevor sat on top of the monkey bars, feet swinging below them. Kix and Drake pushed each other on the merry-go-round, running along the outside then jumping on for the ride while some of the littler kids sat in the center, squealing at them to go faster. Others played on the swings and rode the plastic animal-shaped teeter-totters. No one seemed interested in challenging Payton and Trevor's claimed position above them.

Remembering that Trevor had asked her something, she drew her attention away from her father and said, "What did you say?"

"Your dad." Trevor motioned vaguely toward the couple on the blanket. "He's giving you a little more space. Letting you play tennis with me earlier and now letting us hang out over here on our own without him glaring at me every two minutes."

"Maybe he's starting to trust me a little more," she said with a shrug.

"Or maybe he's getting more interested in flirting

with his new girlfriend than watching his kids," Trevor said with a matter-of-fact shrug. "Been there."

She looked at him from beneath her lashes. "What do you mean?"

"Me and Drake have hardly seen our dad since he got his new girlfriend. Ashlynn," he added, holding cupped hands a significant distance in front of his chest. "Blonde. *Very* blonde. Massive, uh, proportions."

Payton's giggle sounded a little hollow even to her. "Doesn't she like kids?"

Shrugging again, Trevor said, "She likes us okay, I guess. It's just that she and Dad want to spend all their time together without us in their way."

She had already noticed that his mother and stepdad weren't exactly the hands-on type of parents. Trevor and Drake had a great deal of freedom to roam the campgrounds, only checking in occasionally. Was their mother, too, more interested in her new husband than her sons?

She couldn't think of any way to ask without being rude, but she couldn't help wondering.

"My dad's not really like that," she said, shifting her weight on the narrow bar. "He's, like, totally committed to being Superdad. Ever since our mom died, he's been with us almost every minute when he's not working. Kix and I were kind of hoping if he'd find someone nice to date maybe he'd back off a little. And maybe she could be on our side sometimes when his rules get too crazy."

She wasn't comforted by the tone of Trevor's short laugh. "Yeah, Drake and me thought something like that when Mom married Wayne. He seemed cool and we thought since our dad doesn't come around much anymore, maybe Wayne could do guy stuff with us. But he just says he doesn't want to 'overstep his boundaries,' which means he pretty much stays out of anything my mom and dad decide about us."

Payton looked back at her dad and Maggie again. They didn't seem too concerned about what she and Kix were doing at the moment. She watched Maggie laugh at something her dad said, then pat his arm. She looked pretty comfortable touching him. And he seemed happy enough to have her touching him.

"Actually, Ashlynn has gotten pretty bossy lately," Trevor mused. "The more she gets involved with Dad, the more she thinks she's someone else who has the right to tell us what to do. And because she wants to keep him happy, anything he says goes, whether it's stupid or not."

Payton swallowed. "Well, Dad probably won't get together with Maggie, anyway. He's pretty slow when it comes to that sort of thing."

"Well, yeah. And I mean, look at her. She's pretty hot."

Frowning, Payton asked, "Too hot for my dad, you mean?"

"I, uh, didn't say that."

But she thought that was what he'd meant. So maybe Maggie wasn't all that interested in her dad. And maybe, Payton thought, looking at the cozy couple again, that wasn't such a bad thing after all.

Sure, it had been her idea to get them together. Her thought that maybe it would be nice to have an ally, someone who understood fashion and teens and stuff.... But maybe it would be best to just leave things alone for now.

Chapter Eight

Maggie's bedroom was dim, quiet, the sounds from outside muted into a soothing drone. Garrett's heartbeat was still rapid beneath his slightly damp, lightly furred chest. Nestled against him, her head rose and fell with his breathing, a restful, gentle rocking she found all too addicting. She could so get used to this.

She knew he'd have to leave soon. Though she couldn't see her bedside clock from this position, she figured it had to be a little after midnight. He'd want to be back in his cabin before his girls woke for the day, and he needed some sleep himself. But she was reluctant to let him go. For all she knew, this could be the last time she would have him here.

It occurred to her that every time she was with him, she wondered if it would be the last. The lingering question made these interludes bittersweet, but considering her reluctance to insert herself too deeply into his family life, and his to risk letting her, uncertainty was an inherent part of their relationship.

His chest rose again with a deep inhale that he released very slowly. He was probably preparing to leave. For just a moment, her fingers tightened on his shoulder in automatic protest, but she gave in quickly to the inevitable and released her hold.

"I should be getting back," he said, echoing her thoughts. She was gratified to hear the reluctance in his voice. He wanted to stay with her at least a little longer. It was nice to know she wasn't the only one enjoying this sweet stolen interlude.

"I'll miss you." The words escaped her almost before she realized she'd said them aloud.

He pressed his lips to her forehead in a lingering kiss that she chose to interpret as a ditto.

"The girls and I are going for a swim after breakfast, then I promised to take them for a trail ride at the stables down the road from here. After lunch, Kix wants to play at the carnival y'all have advertised and I promised Payton she could hang out with those boys for a while."

She had to smile at his disgruntled tone. "I'm sure she'll appreciate getting to spend one last afternoon with her new friends."

"And that will be the end of her relationship with him." He sounded a little too happy about that.

"Oh, they'll probably friend each other online and stay in touch for a little while, but then it will fade away when they get busy with school and their other friends."

She paused abruptly, wondering if she was foretelling a similar ending to her own affair with Garrett, but because that question made her too uncomfortable, she brushed it away. This was about his daughter, not herself. "Payton will probably have another boyfriend sometime during the coming school year," she predicted.

As for herself—well, she couldn't imagine finding anyone else who made her feel the way Garrett did. Another unsettling thought she tucked away to mull over later.

He scowled. "Great. I'd hoped I had another couple of years before that happened."

"They start earlier these days."

"If she thinks she's going to start dating at thirteen, she is very mistaken. I'll let her hang out with those kids here for a couple hours, but that's only because I'm nearby."

Maggie laughed softly. "My dad always swore Hannah and I wouldn't be allowed to date until we were thirty. Which would mean I still couldn't be seeing you."

That made him frown a bit before he asked, "So when *did* you start dating?"

"Officially? Sixteen."

"What does that mean?"

She smiled. "Maybe I had a couple dates he didn't know about before that. Mom knew, but we decided what Dad didn't know wouldn't hurt him."

Garrett's expression then could best be described as a glower. "I don't like the sound of that."

"Trust me, it was all very innocent. Just hanging out with friends at the movies or the skating rink. Mom didn't let me car date until she thought I was mature enough to handle any situations that might arise. And it was drilled into me from the start that if I ever got into a car with someone who'd been drinking or who tended to drive recklessly to show off to friends, I'd be locked in my room until I was old enough to draw retirement," she added with a laugh. "I knew they exaggerated, of course, but there was just enough doubt that I always followed those rules. Besides, I had enough common sense to have figured that out myself."

"I'm having enough trouble just letting Payton hang out at the tennis court or volleyball courts with a boy. I'll worry about the next step later. Hopefully much later."

She dropped a kiss on his chin. "It'll be okay, Garrett. I turned out all right."

She wanted to believe Payton, too, would survive the turbulent teen years relatively unscathed. She knew Garrett had dedicated himself to making sure of that outcome as best he could, always putting his own desires second to his children's welfare. As intimidated as she was by the thought of such responsibility for herself, she couldn't think of anyone more capable or committed to the task than the strong, sexy man in her bed—for now.

He swept a hand slowly down the length of her body. "You turned out more than all right," he said, his voice deep.

With a little shiver, she arched into his touch and lifted her mouth to his. The kiss quickly grew hot enough to evolve into much more. He shifted his weight, pinning her beneath him for several long, pleasurable minutes that might have stretched into another hour or more had he not determinedly dragged his mouth from hers and disentangled their interlocked limbs. "I really have to go."

She sighed and pushed a strand of hair from her flushed face. "I know."

Magnificently nude and still partially aroused, he climbed from the bed. She took a moment just to admire him before reaching for her robe. She felt his gaze on her when she stretched out her arms to slip into it, and maybe she took her time wrapping it around her. Maybe she wanted to give him just a little reminder of what he was leaving behind.

When he was dressed, she walked him to the door. "Are you working tomorrow?" he asked.

"I work pretty much every day, at least a few hours, unless I make arrangements for someone to fill in for me for a day or two."

"So I'll probably see you around sometime tomorrow, then."

"I'm sure you will."

He reached for the doorknob, then stopped. He spoke without looking at her. "Starting Monday, I'll be back at work full-time. Taking care of the girls after work."

With an effort, she kept her smile in place when she nodded. "Yes, I know."

She hoped he understood that she didn't expect anything from him after this lovely week ended. She knew he'd be busy. As she was herself.

"So, what I'm asking is—maybe we can still get together occasionally? I mean, the girls can stay with Mom for a few extra hours sometimes. You and I could go out for a meal, maybe. Take the Cessna up for a spin. Maybe I could bring takeout and we could eat here."

They could do that, she thought with careful optimism. It would probably be good for the girls to spend a little time away from their father. And for him to have an occasional break from them. No one had to know what he was doing during those breaks, so there would be no reason for anyone to develop unrealistic expectations or conclusions. "Maybe I could cook for you sometime. I make a mean veggie lasagna."

He glanced at her then with a somewhat tentative smile. "I like lasagna."

"We'll do that sometime, then."

"I'd like that."

"So would I."

He looked as though he wanted to kiss her again. Maybe he was afraid of how much longer he would end up staying if he did. Instead, he merely touched her face fleetingly and then let himself out. She locked the door behind him.

This could work, she thought. For a while, at least. After that—well, she didn't want to think that far ahead tonight.

"So, rumor has it you're seeing that good-looking single dad in cabin six."

Maggie looked up from her tablet screen to find four of her employees grinning at her. They sat in her office upstairs in the main building early Saturday for a quick meeting before starting the workday. Located at the back of the building, her office window provided a nice view of the lake and the wooded shore on the other side. The furnishings were simple—a small, functional desk and office chair and a rectangular table with six padded chairs arranged around it, five of those chairs currently occupied by Maggie and her Saturday crew. A coffee carafe and a box of pastries sat in the center of the table and everyone had taken advantage of the availability.

They'd already discussed inventory and maintenance issues and looked at the upcoming week's work schedules. Starting Monday, one of the maids was taking a few days off to visit family, which meant a shift in hours for a couple of others. With the morning's business out of the way, Maggie had asked if anyone had any more questions or items of discussion. Which was when saucy Caroline Churchill had commented about Maggie and Garrett.

"Garrett and I are friends," Maggie said calmly, knowing overreaction would simply fuel rumor. "Now, are there any other—"

"He's the one who plays guitar at Sunday services, right?" Lucia Soto Rivera, who'd worked for the resort since Maggie was in elementary school, inquired.

"Yes. Do I have everyone's supply request forms?"

"I dated a single dad once," Daphne Fernandez mused aloud as she dragged a bite of doughnut through the powdered sugar sprinkled on the paper plate in front of her. Heavyset Daphne, the second-longest in seniority of the staff, had a notorious sweet tooth and could often be found sampling the pie of the day in the diner downstairs when she wasn't diligently cleaning motel rooms or cabins. "A widower with two boys. We were together just long enough for me to get seriously attached to those kids, and then we broke up. I grieved over losing the kids more than I did him. Never saw them again. I heard he got married a couple months after we split, and I'm sure the new wife didn't want his ex hanging around her stepsons. I always wondered if they ever asked about me," she added wistfully.

"I'll bet they did." Lucia heaved a heavy sigh. "I remember when Ray and I broke up, my kids asked about him about a dozen times a day. I hated to tell them he just wasn't interested in seeing them anymore, so I just told them he was on a secret government mission in another country and couldn't come home."

No one laughed. Least of all Maggie.

New employee Darby Burns seemed a little uncertain of the personal direction the conversation had taken, as though she wasn't sure exactly how the boss would take to being teased by the staff. Seeing the hesitation in the younger woman's eyes, Maggie forced a smile. "Enough about my so-called social life. We have a busy day ahead. I'd like to have all the rooms and cabins cleaned by early afternoon, so concentrate on that first and laundry afterward, please."

Daphne crammed the last of the doughnut in her mouth, wiped her lips with a paper napkin and tossed the plate in the trash. She scooped up her coffee cup to take with her when she left. "He is a looker, though," she said to Maggie. "The dad in cabin six, I mean. And I've always had a weakness for a man who can play a guitar. Maybe things would work out better for you and him than they did for me."

Maggie only smiled rather weakly and focused immediately on the job.

Later that busy afternoon, Maggie was leaving the motel headed toward the main building when she spotted Payton and the Ferguson boys getting into a bit of mischief. Her dad and Aaron had been working on putting a new roof on cabin three. They were occupied now with getting the kids' entertainment area set up for the afternoon, scheduled to last from 3:00 until 7:00 p.m. Maggie had noted earlier that they hadn't left the ladder propped against the cabin, but lying nearby with the other supplies they would return to later.

The ladder leaned against the cabin now. Trevor Ferguson sat on top of the roof, knees drawn up in front of him, watching as Payton made her way tentatively up the rungs while Drake stood below and kept a steadying hand on the ladder.

Maggie immediately changed her path to hurry toward the cabin. "Payton, boys, what on earth are you doing?"

Payton startled, but kept her grip on the sides of the metal ladder. "Um…"

"Hi, Miz Bell," Trevor called down from the rooftop. "From up here, we can see all the way to the pavilion. It looks pretty cool."

"I'm sorry, Trevor, but you're going to have to come down. I can't let you kids stay up on the roof."

"It's okay, Miz Bell, we do this all the time at home," Drake assured her earnestly. "We like looking at things from up high. Someday me and Trevor are going to climb a mountain."

"Yes, well, you're not going to climb here. Come down, Payton, and you, too, Trevor."

Payton looked up at Trevor, who shrugged back at her. "What did I tell you?" he muttered.

The girl sighed gustily and backed off the ladder. Maggie thought Payton looked just a little glad to be back on the ground, but that expression was quickly hidden behind a sullen frown. "We would have been fine," Payton said. "It's not much higher than sitting on top of the monkey bars."

Maggie shook her head. "Honestly, Payton, do you really think your father would approve of you climbing a ladder to the top of a roof?"

At the mention of her father, Payton's scowl deepened. "You're going to run and tell him?"

"I'm not running to tell him anything. I have to take care of some things in my office now and then check on the activities at the pavilion. Why don't the three of you head over there? We have free cotton candy and entertainment."

On the ground again now, Trevor rolled his eyes. "Bouncy castles and a cheesy magician? A bunch of rug rats covered in sticky candy and running around on a sugar high? Yeah, sounds great."

"Yeah, great." Payton had the older teen's scornful expression and bored tone down to perfection.

It was probably a good thing the Ferguson boys would be headed back to Bossier City that evening. Payton wouldn't like saying goodbye to her new friends—Trevor, especially—but all in all, Maggie wasn't sure Trevor was the best influence on the girl.

Setting her tablet computer on the picnic table provided for the cabin, she moved to take hold of the ladder. "Trevor, get the other end of this," she instructed. "I want to put it back with the roofing supplies so no one else is tempted to climb it."

"If you want it moved so bad, you can move it yourself." With that, Trevor turned and started walking away, saying over his shoulder, "C'mon, Drake, Payton. We'll take a walk. If boss lady doesn't think *that's* too dangerous for us."

Drake grimaced, but fell into step obediently behind his older brother. Looking a little shocked by her friend's rudeness, Payton hesitated. She took half a step toward Maggie, as though to help with the ladder, but then Trevor called her again. "You coming, Payton?"

"I'll, uh, see you later, Maggie," she muttered, then turned and hurried after the boys.

Disappointed in the girl's choice, Maggie moved the ladder herself, balancing it carefully as she pulled it down and hauled it to the pile of roofing materials. She laid it flat on the ground, then set a few heavy bundles of shingles on top of it to discourage any other aspiring climbers. Her dad didn't usually leave ladders lying around where children could get at them; he must have been called away for a maintenance issue and planned to return soon. She was sure he hadn't imagined that a trio of teens would set the ladder against the cabin and decide to climb up to the roof.

Resuming her walk to the office, she mulled over whether she should mention Payton's escapade to Garrett. Maybe not, she decided. After all, the boys were leaving tonight, so that should be the last of their adventures. And she'd hate to see Garrett crack down on the girl again over such a minor transgression—well, relatively minor, she corrected herself. It could have been very serious had one of the kids fallen and broken a bone, at the least.

Shaking her head, she thought it was a wonder most kids grew up to adulthood. Herself included, she thought, remembering some of her own misadventures. Had to be a constant worry for parents. She couldn't quite explain the root of her own fears of dealing with those issues. Yet just the thought of being responsible for innocent, vulnerable lives—say, Payton and Kix, for example—filled her with dread. She was totally unqualified, lacked any training for such a crucial undertaking. How would she know what to do in an emergency? What to say to soothe their fears or give them guidance? What if her own ignorance caused them irreparable harm, either physical or emotional?

Did Hannah and Andrew already fret about baby Claire's future teen rebellions? Were they preparing themselves already for any eventualities and if so, how? She knew her aunt and uncle still worried themselves half-sick over their grown, now-married daughter Lori. Would she ever have the courage to take on that commitment responsibility herself?

Half an hour later she approached the festivities on the pavilion lawn, noting in satisfaction that the end-of-the-holiday-weekend celebration seemed to be going well. While parents watched and visited, children romped around the playground and stood in line for the three inflatable bouncers, the merry-go-round, tilt-a-whirl and free cotton candy. A "duck pond" sat in the center of the pavilion, consisting of a large round metal tub filled with water in which floated dozens of multicolored rubber duckies. Children were allowed to choose a duck, then received the prize correlated to the number written on the bottom. The small plastic toys and beanbag animals given out as prizes seemed to please the kids she watched play the game. Many of them were dressed in swimsuits, indicating that water sports were a part of the day's plans.

"I don't know about you, but I'm ready for this holiday weekend to be over."

Maggie turned to find her grandmother behind her. "It's gone well, though," she pointed out. "We've had lots of visitors from the surrounding towns and I've talked to several people during the past couple of days who said they'd like to come back and rent a cabin or stay in the campgrounds. The marina, store and diner have all done extra business this week. Two future brides have checked out the pavilion as a potential location for autumn weddings—you know Hannah wants to boost our reputation as a wedding venue. All in all, it seems the weekend festivities have been successful."

"I hope so," Mimi grumbled. "I'd hate to think we've spent more money putting it on than we'll get back in extra business."

"You'd have to talk to Shelby about the numbers, of course, but I think she'll tell us that we've almost broken even this weekend. So if we get extra business in the future from our efforts, then it will all pay off. If not—well, it was worth a shot."

"There's some business I'd just as soon not have," her grandmother muttered, looking over Maggie's shoulder.

Sensing whom she would see behind her, Maggie turned her head. She spotted Garrett first, with a strong jolt of purely physical reaction. With Kix and his mother following close behind, he accompanied his grandmother, who made good progress toward the festivities with her walker. It was the first time Maggie had seen Esther at one of the scheduled events. She wondered if the family had pressured her to come with them today just to get her out of her chair for an hour or so.

"Be nice, Mimi," she said automatically. "She's not your old foe today, she's a paying guest of the resort."

"I know how to do my job," her grandmother retorted. And with that, she swept toward the little group, making Maggie hurry to keep up, a little concerned about what would happen next.

"Good afternoon, everyone," Mimi sang out in a voice coated with sugar. "I hope you've enjoyed your stay so far at our resort. We've had quite a lot of excitement here the past couple of days with all the festivities. I've been so busy with all our many guests that I've hardly had time to speak to everyone."

Maggie didn't quite roll her eyes in response to the blatant boasting, but it wasn't easy to refrain from doing so. What was it about Esther Lincoln that brought out the absolute worst in her usually sweet-natured grandmother? She remembered her grandfather confiding that both Mimi and Esther secretly enjoyed the sparring, but it seemed a bit hard to believe.

"We've had a good enough time," Esther replied

grudgingly. "Considering all the noise and hubbub, of course. Generally I prefer my vacations to be somewhat quieter and with a few more luxuries."

Maggie interceded quickly before verbal jabs turned to physical punches. Not that she thought the two great-grandmothers would actually wrestle on the ground—but she wasn't putting it past them at this point, either, she thought wryly.

"Kix, be sure and get some cotton candy," she urged. "And maybe you'd like to get your face painted? My friend Elisa is under the pavilion with her face-painting supplies and she does some really cute designs for all ages."

"That sounds like fun!" Kix abandoned her grandmother and attached herself to Maggie's side. "Will you go with me to help me pick a design?"

"Of course." Maggie closed her fingers around the girl's when Kix reached for her hand. Fortunately Mimi had already moved on, making a show of graciously acknowledging other guests. Garrett was settling his mother and grandmother into folding chairs to people-watch for a while.

As usual, Kix started chattering immediately, telling Maggie all about her adventures in the lake with her dad that morning. "We swam a long way. Daddy said I'm getting better and better at swimming and he taught me the breaststroke and backstroke. I'm not very good at the backstroke, but he said I just need a little more practice so I told him maybe we could swim here every weekend this summer, since we come for sunrise services anyway, but he said he can't swim every Sunday because he has other things to do sometimes, but we can go to the pool closer to our house more often if I want to. I like it better here but the pool's okay, too. What pattern do you think I should get on my face? I like that one girl's kitten nose and whiskers over there—do you think she could do something like that for me, maybe?"

Maggie smiled. "I'm sure she can."

"Payton will probably make fun of me." Kix's tone was matter-of-fact. "She'll say face painting is for little kids, but I think it's kind of fun. It's whimsical," she added with a rush of inspiration.

"That's exactly what it is," Maggie agreed. "Maybe I'll have mine painted, too."

Kix giggled. "Awesome."

Fifteen minutes later both Kix and Maggie sported facial art—Kix looking like an adorable kitten and Maggie with a ladybug flying on her cheek. Elisa was amused by Kix's breathless babbling and pleased with the girl's excitement over seeing the final results in a hand mirror.

"She's adorable," Elisa said to Maggie. "You're dating her dad?"

"Her dad and I are friends," Maggie answered easily.

Elisa glanced at Garrett, who had approached to admire Kix's face paint. "Good-looking guy," she said beneath her breath. "Nice kid. Maybe you should hold on to that one. Or if not, stand out of the way and let some of us others have a shot at him."

Maggie forced a laugh. "I'll consider your advice."

A little boy of perhaps six bounced impatiently nearby. "Can you make me look like a tiger?" he asked Elisa. "A really scary tiger?"

Elisa winked at Maggie before turning to her new client. "Of course I can. Hop right up in this chair and sit still for me and I'll transform you into the fiercest tiger in the whole resort."

"Cool," the boy said and squirmed into the chair facing Elisa's as Maggie rejoined Kix and Garrett.

"Daddy likes my face paint," Kix reported. "He said I look cute. Didn't you, Daddy?"

"I did." Grinning, he touched a finger lightly to Maggie's cheek, just below the slightly itchy ladybug. "And so do you."

"Why, thank you, sir," she teased. "What about you? Want to get in line? I'm sure Elisa can turn you into a scary tiger. Or a cute kitten."

Kix laughed. "Maybe Daddy could be a clown, like that boy over there."

"I think I'll just stick with the face I've got," Garrett said quickly. "I'm sure it's scary enough."

Kix dissolved into giggles again when her dad made a silly face to go with his words, and Maggie couldn't help laughing herself.

The woman working the duck pond game was a friend of Rosie's who'd been hired to help out for the day. Maggie didn't know her; Hannah and Shelby had made all the arrangements for that day's activities, including hiring the entertainment. The woman motioned toward them. "Bring your daughter over for a prize," she called out cheerfully. "We have something for all ages."

Kix covered her mouth with a laugh. "She thinks you're my mother, Maggie."

"Um, yes." Maggie avoided Garrett's eyes. "Go pick a duck, Kix, and claim your prize. Then maybe you'd like to get some cotton candy. And the magician starts a new performance in just fifteen minutes, you'd probably enjoy that."

In her disconcertion, she was babbling almost as much as Kix, she realized with a little grimace. Kix didn't seem to notice anything awry as she skipped over to the duck pond to join a few other kids, most younger, a couple close to her own age.

"She's having a good time," Maggie commented lightly to Garrett just to fill the sudden silence between them. "And she really does look adorable in her face paint."

"Yeah. I'm glad she's content with just being a kid for a little while longer, at least." Garrett pushed a hand through his hair and glanced around the crowded area, and Maggie knew he was thinking about his older daughter.

To distract him, she pointed to the largest of the inflatable bouncers, one shaped like a fortress. "She'd probably like to jump on that one. I see several kids close to her age in there."

"No doubt," he agreed. "One thing Kix has in abundance is energy to burn."

Maggie shared a smile with him. "I noticed."

Something made her glance to her right at that moment. She spotted Payton standing not far away, frowning back at her while the Ferguson brothers hovered nearby. Was Payton still annoyed about being ordered off the ladder, or was something else bothering her now?

Kix pelted back in their direction, now holding a beanbag toy that vaguely resembled an otter. Or was it a ferret? "Hey, Payton, where've you been? Look at what I won at the duck pond. Sweet, huh? And I got my face painted. Daddy said it was cute. Maggie got a ladybug on her cheek, and he said she looked cute, too. And the lady at the duck pond thought Maggie was my mother, isn't that funny?"

Her eyes narrowed, Payton looked down her nose

at her younger sister. "You're too old for face paint and kiddie games."

"No, I'm not," Kix replied serenely. "I'm having fun. And I'm going to jump on a bouncer and have cotton candy and that will be fun, too. So there. Want to jump with me, Drake?"

The younger of the Ferguson brothers looked somewhat longingly at the kids bouncing and squealing in the inflatables. "Well…"

"Of course he doesn't," Trevor snapped. "Drake's not a little kid, are you, Drake?"

"Uh, no," Drake replied immediately, imitating his brother's look of bored superiority. "I'm too old for bouncing."

His eyes on Payton, Garrett asked, "Maybe we could head over to the diner for ice cream in a few minutes? I'm sure Grammy and Meemaw would enjoy that."

"I don't really want any ice cream," Payton answered. "Me and Trevor and Drake are going to walk through the campgrounds, okay? They're leaving after dinner and we want to take one last walk around the resort. I guess you don't want to go with us, Kix?"

"I want to stay with Dad and Maggie."

"Fine. Okay if I go, Dad?" Payton asked again.

After only a momentary hesitation, he nodded. "I want you back by six-thirty. That's just over an hour. We'll need to start getting ready for dinner not long after that."

She nodded without looking directly at him and headed off toward the campgrounds with her friends. The younger brother looked over his shoulder somewhat wistfully at the festivities they were leaving behind, but Trevor gave him a slight push and the three disappeared into the crowd.

Kix shook her head with a slight huff of disapproval. "Well, I'm going to bounce," she announced defiantly. "I can still be a kid if I want to, right, Daddy?"

He ruffled her hair. "Absolutely. Heck, I'd get in there and bounce with you if they'd let me."

"So would I," Maggie agreed. "Don't be in too much of a hurry to grow up, Kix. Take time to just enjoy playing and laughing."

Kix threw her arms around Maggie's waist. "I love you, Maggie."

Both startled and touched, Maggie patted the girl's back. "I love you, too, Kix. Want me to hold your otter while you bounce?"

Kix looked at the cheap toy with a tilted head. "It's an otter? Oh, I thought it was a weiner dog."

Maggie laughed softly. "I guess it's whatever you want it to be."

"I'll decide later." Kix handed her the toy. "I'm going to go bounce now, then I want to see the magician. I love magic shows. And cotton candy—I love cotton candy, too."

Kix loved a lot of things, Maggie reflected as the girl dashed away at her usual warp speed. Which didn't make her any less moved by having been on the receiving end of the girl's warm affection.

"She's crazy about you, you know," Garrett murmured in her ear.

She glanced up at him, her smile feeling a little tremulous. "She really is a sweet girl. Both your daughters are, even if Payton's going through a little rebellion right now."

"I'm just glad those boys are leaving the resort this evening," he said gruffly. "I'm hoping once she's out of their influence things will be a little easier."

Thinking of the way Trevor seemed to be increasingly egging on Payton's mutiny, Maggie said, "I hope so, too."

"I think I'll take some cotton candy to Mom and Meemaw. They'd probably enjoy the treat."

"I'll just wait here for Kix and then we'll join you."

He touched her painted cheek again with a little chuckle. "Ladybugs look good on you."

"Thanks," she quipped. "I'll keep that in mind for my next formal event."

His gaze lingered on her smiling mouth for several long moments during which she suspected he was thinking about kissing her—or was that merely a projection of her own wishes? And then he dropped his hand, moving back to put a discreet distance between them. "I'll, um, see you in a few minutes."

She nodded, then watched him walk toward the pavilion. She really loved watching him walk with that slight military swagger. She loved the way he looked with the sunlight in his crisp brown hair. She loved…

…entirely too much about him, actually.

She hadn't really been foolish enough to fall in love with Garrett McHale, had she?

Her heart stumbling in midbeat, she drew a sharp breath, then turned again to watch his daughter play.

Chapter Nine

Six-thirty came and went without sign of Payton. Maggie had spent that hour with Garrett and his family, enjoying the magic show, eating snacks, watching Kix play at the carnival. Kix now possessed a pink balloon poodle in addition to her otter/weiner dog. Her face paint was a little smeared after her vigorous jumping sessions and her bright red hair curled riotously around her flushed face. She looked a little tired and a lot happy.

She'd stayed close to Maggie's side all afternoon, holding her hand, occasionally hugging her, making her affection clear in her innocently demonstrative way. As much as Maggie enjoyed spending the pleasant afternoon with the girl—and her father—it worried her a bit that Kix seemed to be so attached to her, especially in light of the conversation her coworkers had shared that morning about dating single dads.

At six-forty, Garrett scowled at his watch. "Damn it."

His mother cleared her throat loudly, looking pointedly at Kix.

Garrett sighed. "Sorry, Mom. But I told Payton to be back by six-thirty and she's ten minutes late."

"Give her another five minutes," his grandmother advised. "She's probably just lost track of time."

"If she's not back pretty soon, I'm going looking for her."

"Probably should," his grandmother agreed.

Was Payton being deliberately late? Maggie glanced around the clearing grounds, wondering if this was yet another minirebellion. It wasn't quite time to worry, but if the girl didn't show up soon, she wouldn't be able to help it.

By seven, Garrett was clearly angry with his older daughter, the rest of his family was in dread of the coming confrontation and Maggie was rather wishing she could slip quietly away before it occurred. She knew Payton would be humiliated if her father chewed her out in front of Maggie, but Garrett was in no mood to be patient and discreet. Because his grandmother looked tired, Maggie offered to take her back to the cabin in a golf cart while Garrett found his daughter, an offer both Esther and Paulette accepted. Garrett told Kix to go with the women and start washing up for dinner.

"I'll find your sister and bring her back," he added grimly.

Kix sighed heavily. "I'm glad I'm not Payton," she whispered loudly to Maggie.

Fifteen minutes later, Maggie returned to the pavilion area where the inflatables were being taken down and the other entertainment supplies packed away. She wasn't sure Garrett would still be there, rather than scouring the resort for signs of Payton and the boys, but she saw him standing near the pavilion talking with Trevor and Drake's mom. The expression on his face had her climbing out of the golf cart and hurrying toward him.

He turned when she approached. "Do you have a procedure in place here to look for missing kids?" he asked her, his voice tight.

Swallowing hard, she nodded. "No one has seen them?"

"No. The boys were supposed to be back at the same time as Payton." He nodded toward the Alexanders, who looked almost as worried as Garrett. "They wanted the boys to help them load up at seven. Trevor told them he'd be back by then. He carries a cell phone, but he isn't answering. Payton doesn't have hers with her. She forgot to charge it last night and the battery is dead. Wayne just drove all through the resort, but he didn't see them."

Maggie pulled her phone out of her pocket. "I'll get everyone out looking for them."

Garrett nodded. "Mind if I borrow your golf cart? I'm going to start looking myself."

"I'll come with you." Dialing her dad's number, she hurried after Garrett to the cart, making a mental list of all the places three teenagers could hide in the resort. Yet she couldn't imagine that Payton would be deliberately evading attention. As annoyed as the girl was with her father, it seemed unlikely that Payton would think hiding would accomplish anything. More likely the three had settled in somewhere to talk and had lost track of time—which didn't explain why Trevor wasn't answering his phone.

Another hour passed. Along with every member of the resort staff, Maggie and Garrett had combed through the place looking for the missing trio. Maggie remembered several good hiding places from her own youth, but they were all empty. A team had been dispatched to search the old, no-longer-used road that led from the area behind the family housing compound to the highway. It wasn't well-known, and both ends were blocked with cables, but there was always the possibility the kids had discovered the road and decided to explore it and the surrounding woods. Though shadows were beginning to deepen beneath the heavily leafed trees, searchers moved through the woods, calling the teens' names.

Another search team scoured the lake's shoreline, looking for any evidence that Payton and the boys had gone into the water. Shoes or articles of clothing on the shore, perhaps, a sight that would strike fear into all their hearts. Fortunately, nothing was found to indicate they had decided to take an unsupervised swim.

While Bryan, Aaron, Andrew and Shelby organized a thorough sweep of every campsite, cabin, motel room and structure in the resort, Maggie and Garrett returned to his cabin to give his worried family an update. Maggie wasn't particularly surprised to find her mother, her aunt Sarah and her grandmother there, offering reassurance and comfort to Paulette, Esther and Kix. The silly old feud was pushed aside when a true crisis erupted, when a child's safety was in doubt. Even as Maggie and Garrett entered the cabin, they saw Mimi handing a cup of tea to Esther, who accepted it with a nod of thanks. Sarah sat on the couch next to a visibly distraught Paulette while Linda was in the kitchen with Kix, keeping the child busy assembling sandwiches from supplies she must have brought from the store.

Everyone looked around hopefully when Maggie

and Garrett walked in, only to sag in disappointment at what they saw on their faces. Garrett shook his head in response to his mother's questioning look. "No sign yet. I'm going back out to look again, but I wanted to make sure everyone's okay here."

"We're fine," his grandmother said firmly, giving her less resilient daughter a bracing look. "I'm sure those kids are okay, they're just into mischief somewhere. Dixie was just telling me some of the stunts her grandson Steven got into when he was growing up here. I guess spending so much time in a vacation spot makes kids think the usual rules don't apply."

Maggie half expected her grandmother to retort that Steven had certainly had rules to follow, which he had obeyed most of the time. But apparently Mimi understood that Esther's tone was sharpened by fear, so she held her tongue—for now. Maggie suspected the bickering would resume once Payton was safely returned—as Maggie believed she would be. Apparently Pop had been right that Mimi and Esther actually enjoyed their caustic interactions.

"Has anyone called the police?" Sarah asked quietly after a quick glance toward the kitchen and Kix. "It's possible they left the resort, you know. Maybe they're trying to make some sort of statement by running away."

"I think Dad's taking care of all that," Maggie replied.

Garrett's phone rang and everyone froze while he answered it. Standing closest to him, Maggie felt her heart stop at the look in his eyes when he responded with monosyllables, then slowly lowered his phone. She rested a hand on his arm, feeling the muscles as rigid as steel there.

"What?" she asked in a voice barely over a whisper.

He looked down at her. "The Alexanders just discovered that their boat is missing from its slip in the marina. Searchers are going out on the lake now looking for the boat."

Paulette gave a hard gasp. Maggie grimaced. "I never even thought of looking for a boat," she admitted.

Garrett's jaw was set in a hard line of anger and worry. "I was told the marina and the main building were searched earlier. I didn't know the Alexanders had a boat there, and I certainly wasn't told it was missing. They said they didn't even think to look."

Paulette twisted her hands in her lap. "You don't really think they've taken the boat out by themselves?"

Peering over the bar that separated the kitchen from the main room, Kix piped up. "Trevor knows how to drive his family's boat. He bragged about it a lot."

"Could they really have gotten the boat out of the slip without anyone seeing them?" Esther asked, her face deeply creased with concern.

"I suppose it's possible," Maggie conceded reluctantly. "If Uncle C.J. was busy with other customers and no one else happened to be around for a few minutes, they could have gotten away without attracting attention."

"Oh, my God," Paulette moaned. "And now it's getting dark. What if...?"

"Don't start borrowing trouble, Paulette," her mother ordered. "They'll be fine."

Maggie gave a slight tug at Garrett's arm. "I realize the search teams are already out, but I know this lake like the back of my hand. I've grown up here, after all. We can use one of the resort boats at the marina."

Her mother looked toward the big glass door at the back of the cabin. "It's getting dark."

"We'll be careful," Maggie promised. Though she preferred boating in the daytime, she'd been out on the lake after dark many times using running lights and spotlights. At least there was little wind this evening and the water was smooth, she thought, desperately hoping the kids were safe in a cove somewhere.

Garrett moved toward the door. "We'll keep in touch," he said over his shoulder to their anxious family members.

He beat her to the driver's side of the golf cart, so she climbed into the passenger's seat. "I can't believe Payton would do this," he said as he guided the cart toward the marina. "What was she thinking?"

"I doubt that she was thinking at all. If she's gone out in the boat with the boys, it was either to prove something to them or to make a statement to you. And she was angry with me," Maggie added.

She'd already told him about her confrontation with Payton and the boys when she'd insisted on looking on the roof of cabin two earlier. They weren't there, but she'd had to explain to Garrett why she'd thought to look there. She'd downplayed the kids' rudeness to her, saying merely that they'd been unhappy with her for ordering them down. As she'd expected, he had not been pleased that Payton had attempted such a foolish stunt.

"I should have been watching her more closely," he muttered, his hands tight on the cart steering wheel. "I gave her too much freedom too soon. Let myself be distracted by...well, I should have paid more attention."

Maggie frowned. "Garrett, this is not your fault." Or hers, either, she added silently, even though something in his tone made her feel vaguely guilty. "You've been very vigilant. Payton simply slipped away from you this time."

He wouldn't meet her gaze. "I let down my guard."

Twisting her fingers in her lap, she subsided into silent worry and self-blame. Maybe she shouldn't have distracted Garrett from his parenting, even though she'd thought he needed time for himself. Maybe she should have told him earlier about Payton's escapade with the ladder. She'd thought she was doing them both a favor by keeping the incident to herself, but maybe if she'd interceded more...

In the deepening twilight, she spotted a small crowd milling around the marina and she recognized the boys' mother and stepfather among them. The stepdad appeared to be angrily confronting Maggie's uncle C.J. Surely he wasn't blaming C.J. when Trevor and Drake had been allowed to run unsupervised all around the resort for their entire stay?

She was already mapping her search path of the lake in her head when she and Garrett climbed out of the cart. She'd coordinate with the other search teams, of course, staying in constant touch with their phones. Payton and the boys would be safely returned to their families; she refused to accept any other outcome for this ordeal.

She and Garrett had just stepped onto the dock behind the marina when Garrett's phone rang again. He lifted it to his ear to answer. Moments later she saw a deep breath shake his entire body.

"Thank you," he said into the phone. "I'll be waiting at the marina."

She heard another phone ring, heard the boys' mother give a loud gasp followed by a fervent "thank God."

Garrett lowered his phone to his side as if it had suddenly become almost too heavy to support. His eyes met Maggie's. "They've been found," he said, though she'd already reached that conclusion. "They're safe."

She wrapped her arms around his waist and hugged him tightly, her relief almost overwhelming. "I'm so glad."

His arms enclosed her so fiercely she could hardly breathe—not that she was complaining. And then he stiffened a bit and set her carefully away from him. She couldn't read his expression when he said, "That was your dad who called. A couple of fishermen returning to their dock found the Alexanders' boat adrift in a cove on the far end of the lake. One of the rescuers is a friend of your dad's, so he called him as soon as the kids identified themselves. They were lost and out of gas, but they're safe. The boat's being towed back here."

"I'm so glad they're safe," Maggie breathed, swiping at a tear that leaked from her left eye. "When I heard the boat was missing..."

He drew a sharp breath and looked toward the activity on the pier where the people milling around were hugging each other and high-fiving in celebration. "I need to call my mom."

"Of course." Because he seemed to want her to, she moved back a few steps to give him privacy to make that grateful call.

Ten minutes later the rescue boat chugged into the marina towing the second boat. Wayne and Melanie Alexander surged forward and started yelling at the boys before the boat was even tied up. Staying a couple of steps behind Garrett, Maggie moved toward the boat, noting that Payton looked pale and subdued in the now mostly artificial light. Had the girl been crying? Her face looked a little splotchy.

C.J. reached down into the boat to lift Payton out and set her on the pier. While the boys' angry mother and stepfather continued to reprimand them, Payton looked tentatively up at her dad.

"Are you really mad?" she asked in an unsteady voice.

"Yes," he answered simply, then swept her into his arms and buried his face in her tousled auburn hair. Payton promptly burst into tears. Maggie had to swipe both hands across her own damp eyes.

She realized at that moment that she'd never been so worried in her life. She could hardly imagine what Garrett had been going through since the discovery that his daughter was missing.

It was late that evening when Garrett stood outside Maggie's door, but he knew she was still awake. He could see lights in several of her windows and could hear the faint strains of music through the front door. Lights were on in the neighboring homes, too, but no one stirred outside except Steven's old yellow Lab, who had already ambled up for an ear rub.

Hands in his pockets, he stared at Maggie's door, trying to decide whether to knock. Maybe he'd just head back to the cabin and talk to her tomorrow. He wasn't sure what he was doing here anyway.

The door opened and Maggie leaned against the jamb, her arms crossed over her chest as she studied him. "Do you want to come in or did you just come to stand on my porch?" she asked lightly.

Did she know exactly how long he'd been standing there deliberating? A little abashed by his uncharacteristic indecision, he cleared his throat. "I was just about to knock."

She moved back. "Come in, Garrett."

After only a momentary hesitation, he stepped inside.

She closed the door behind him. "How's Payton?"

"Asleep. She was worn out after that adventure."

"I'm sure she was."

Maggie had hung around long enough to know that Payton had been badly shaken by being lost and then stranded on the lake in the boat. Payton swore that she'd only intended to sit in the boat and talk with the boys, but Trevor and Drake had conspired to cast off and take the boat out before Payton could do anything to stop them. Trevor had wanted to show off his rebellious side and his boating skills, both aimed at impressing Payton on their last evening together. Rather than being impressed, she'd been frightened when he first got lost on the big lake and then ran out of gas as darkness began to fall. She'd envisioned either spending a long, dark night adrift on the lake or possibly hitting an unseen obstacle and capsizing.

Payton had known her family would be worried sick about her and that she would be in trouble with her father, so all in all it had been a miserable ordeal for her. Even though Garrett had let her know he was not happy with her for getting into the boat with the boys in the first place—something she had to have known he would disapprove of—he'd gone relatively easy on her because she had been so upset. She was, of course, forbidden to have anything more to do with the Ferguson brothers, though that wouldn't be a significant issue because the Alexanders had packed up and pulled out not long after the boat and boys were returned. Garrett had been tempted to do the same, but his mother and grandmother were too tired and drained by the worry of the afternoon to deal with packing and cleanup. They would stick with the plan and leave tomorrow morning. He, for one, would be glad when this vacation was over.

Though there was one aspect of the holiday he would miss, he thought as he studied Maggie's somber expression. His palms itched with the urge to cup her face between them. His lips throbbed with a need to be pressed against hers. Every hard inch of him ached with hunger for her.

He kept his hands in his pockets, a good distance of floor between them.

"So we're leaving tomorrow," he said, not quite meeting her eyes. "Pretty early, I think. The weather service is predicting thunderstorms to roll in late morning, so I'd like to get home ahead of them. I told Jay I'd play for the service, but we're cutting out almost as soon as it's over."

She nodded as if she'd expected something like this. "I'm sure you're ready to get back to your usual routines."

"Yeah. Maybe a week was too long for a family vacation. I thought it would help me bond a little better with the girls, but it seems to have done the opposite."

"Kix has had a great time," she reminded him. "This was the way she wanted to spend her birthday week."

"I should have packed up and headed home when Payton started acting up a couple days ago. I suspected those boys were a bad influence, but I just kept giving her more leeway."

Now he wondered if his lenience had been for Payton's sake—or if he'd been so distracted by his deepening attraction to Maggie that he'd neglected the signs that Payton was pushing too far beyond the limits he'd set. He should have known he couldn't juggle his family responsibilities with a relationship, even the casual, no-strings affair Maggie seemed to envision for them. And the past week hadn't even included his job obligations.

"She looked pretty scared when she came back to the marina. And very happy to see you," Maggie pointed out. "Maybe she learned a lesson about letting friends lead her into risky situations."

"I hope so. I'll be keeping a close eye on her to be sure." He drew a deep breath before adding, "That me time you kept talking about? Guess that had better wait for a while longer."

Her expression told him she got his message. "You have to do what you think is best for your kids, of course."

Even at the cost of his own desires. The words hovered unsaid but understood between them. "That's what I think is best."

She nodded in apparent resignation. Had he hoped she would protest? That she would at least look disappointed? He hadn't wanted to hurt her, but maybe he'd have liked to think he meant enough to her that she'd be just a little saddened by his decision. If she was, she hid it well.

Maybe this last stunt of Payton's had convinced Maggie that she was better off staying out of the single-dad drama. She could probably spend her own me time with her choice of footloose, commitment-free men. And while he wouldn't trade places with any of those guys if it meant giving up his girls, he would miss spending time with Maggie. He knew the heated, intimate images that flitted through his head with that thought would replay in more vivid detail in the weeks of lonely nights to come.

All of which made his voice gruffer than he intended

when he took a step backward toward the door and said, "I'd better go."

Again, she made no effort to argue. "All right. I'll see you at service in the morning. And if you need any help packing up or checking out, just let me know."

He nodded shortly. "Yeah. Thanks. For everything."

"You're welcome. Good night, Garrett."

It sounded more like goodbye than good night—but maybe that was just his imagination. "Good night, Maggie."

Did his sound the same to her? For only a moment, he thought he might have seen regret cross her face, but she schooled it immediately.

He would have liked to kiss her one last time—but because he feared where that might lead, considering his willpower around her had always been shaky at best, he merely reached for the door and let himself out.

It was a long, dark walk back to the cabin. Ignoring the various sounds from the campgrounds, he concentrated only on the crunching of his own feet on the pavement and the guttural curses that occasionally escaped him along the way.

The thunderstorm that had been predicted for midmorning hit earlier than expected and with a vengeance, booming across the lake, rattling windows, washing the resort with a torrential downfall of heavy rain. Summer storms weren't unusual in this part of the state, but they were almost always impressive. It was understood that the sunrise service was canceled in case of bad weather, so Maggie didn't bother braving the weather to go to the pavilion. She knew her dad and Aaron would be patrolling in slickers and golf carts to make sure their guests were safe in the storm, and she trusted that they would use proper precautions in the wind and lightning.

She made herself a cup of strong black tea and some toast and ate at her table, watching the trees behind her trailer bowing in the almost horizontally blowing rain. Vague metaphors of supple trees bending but not breaking flitted through her mind; she could probably apply them to herself, but she just wasn't in the mood for philosophy at the moment. She'd rather indulge in a little pity party this morning. She promised herself she wouldn't let it last long. Still, falling head over heels for the wrong man did seem to call for at least a brief period of sadness. She didn't know if her heart was broken, but it was certainly cracked. She could feel the waves of pain radiating from the wound.

She'd known better, she reminded herself. From the beginning. Garrett hadn't had time for a dalliance with her, and she had so little else to offer him. They couldn't be more wrong for each other—but they had felt so very right together.

The rain stopped at just before noon, leaving glittering puddles and a clean, fresh scent in its wake. Campers and other guests reemerged from their various shelters, some heading for the water, many packing up and leaving at the end of their holiday weekends. Maggie had a few things to attend to at the motel, which she handled swiftly and efficiently. Only then did she check cabin six.

The cabin was empty, left spotlessly clean as if her cleaning crew had just been through it. There was no sign left that Garrett's family had ever stayed there.

They didn't live far away, of course. They would be back for Sunday services, if not for play days at the resort. But though she would continue to smile and chat and interact pleasantly with them, nothing between them would ever be quite the same. With that thought, she felt the painful cracks in her heart widen just a bit more deeply.

Though Sundays were usually light workdays for her, she threw herself into her job that afternoon, very much needing the distraction from her thoughts.

A busy week followed, the summer season now at its peak. The resort was filled almost to capacity even without the hoopla of the Independence Day events—all of which had been deemed successful, though the family agreed next year's celebration could use some tweaking. Steven returned to his firefighting job, Hannah and Andrew took the baby back to their home and obligations in Dallas and life went on much like any other hot, busy summer in Maggie's lifetime here. She did not hear from Garrett during that week—not that she'd expected to, she told herself.

For the first time in her almost thirty years, she found herself wondering about life outside the resort gate. Should she consider following the example set by Steven and Hannah and Lori, venturing out into the world to explore a new and different life? Was there something out there to fill this sudden emptiness inside her?

She braced herself to see Garrett and his family at services Sunday morning, assuring herself she would be able to carry on as if nothing had changed between them. She hoped Payton had gotten over her irritation about the ladder incident and her embarrassment about the boating misadventure so they could chat comfortably after the service as they had in the past. She would ask about Kix's kitten; surely that would initiate an innocuous conversation.

Yet when Jay stood to open the service at seven sharp, the McHale family was nowhere to be seen. A young man with rather stringy blond hair, a smattering of acne and a shy smile sat at Jay's side with a battered electric guitar plugged into a small, portable amp.

"Our usual accompanist, Garrett McHale, couldn't be with us this morning because of illness in his family," Jay announced, his gaze pausing for a moment on Maggie as he glanced over the small crowd gathered beneath the pavilion on this bright, early Sunday. "I persuaded a talented young friend, Kyle Snow, to fill in. Let's all welcome Kyle with a big amen, shall we?"

Chuckling, the little congregation obliged by saying "amen" in unison. Kyle blushed a little, ducking his head to let his hair fall over his face. He strummed quietly along as Jay led the group in the first song, a familiar hymn they sang to lyrics projected on a portable screen set up to one side of the pavilion. Maggie added her voice to the chorus, but she couldn't help fretting about the illness in Garrett's family. Was someone really sick, or was it merely an excuse to avoid returning to the resort so soon? Would they ever feel truly comfortable here again?

After delivering his usual upbeat, encouraging sermon, Jay closed the service as he always did with a song and a prayer and an invitation to his little church in town. Afterward, he lingered to shake hands and exchange greetings with the attendees. Maggie held back until nearly everyone else had drifted away. Only then did she approach Jay, who smiled and held out a hand to her. She returned his warm handshake and complimented him on his sermon before asking a little too casually, "Did you say someone in Garrett's family is ill?"

Jay nodded. "Several of them, apparently. Some sort

of bug. I asked if he needed help, but he said he had everything under control."

"Of course he does," she murmured, thinking that Garrett would say that, regardless.

"So have you heard from him since they left last week?" Jay's tone was as studiously nonchalant as her own, suggesting he knew something had gone on between her and Garrett even if he didn't know details. That didn't surprise her, considering that Jay was Garrett's longtime closest friend, but she would bet there was plenty Garrett had left unsaid.

"No," she said. "I haven't."

Jay nodded as if he'd expected that reply. "He tends to get…overwhelmed sometimes. It would be good for him to have someone to vent to occasionally. Someone who cares about him enough to provide moral support when he needs it."

"I'm glad he has you to turn to for that," she said evenly, her hands clenching behind her.

Jay's smile was endearingly lopsided. "I don't think I'm exactly what he needs in his life, though I do my best to give him encouragement when I can."

"I think that's all he wants right now."

"Do you?"

Looking away from the pastor's kind blue eyes with their echoes of old pain of his own, she cleared her throat. "It would take someone very special to offer him more."

Jay reached out to squeeze her shoulder lightly. "Don't underestimate yourself, Maggie Bell. I believe you are as special as you choose to be."

He was giving her credit for more courage than she thought she possessed. But that seemed to be Jay's special gift—an unflagging belief in others that made them want to prove him right.

Still, his words stayed with her the rest of that day and haunted her during the long, restless night. She woke Monday morning with a vague thought of perhaps calling Garrett sometime in the coming weeks with a friendly, informal invitation to a movie or a night out for music and drinks. Maybe with some of her other friends. All very casual and uncomplicated, no strings to entangle either of them. Just a pleasant refuge from responsibility. It was the least she could offer—or should she say it was the most? Whichever, maybe Garrett would appreciate the thought behind it.

Her cell phone rang early Monday afternoon just as she'd finished placing an order for new linens. She glanced at the screen, then felt her heart stutter in response to seeing Garrett's name there. So much for the courage she thought she'd mustered during the night.

"Hello?"

"Maggie?" Rather than Garrett's deep tone, it was a high-pitched, quavering voice she heard. "It's Kix. I'm using Daddy's phone."

Hearing the tears clogging the girl's throat, Maggie spoke urgently. "Kix? Sweetie, what's wrong?"

"Everyone's sick. Payton and Grammy and Daddy and me, too. Daddy's trying to take care of us all but he's really sick. He doesn't know I'm calling you, but I knew you'd want me to. Was I right?" she asked less confidently.

"You were absolutely right," Maggie said firmly. "Sit tight, honey. I'm on my way."

Kix heaved a deep sigh of relief into the phone. "I'm glad."

Reaching for her keys, Maggie hoped Garrett would be glad. But regardless, she was going to help. He and the girls needed her.

Chapter Ten

Kix must have been watching out the front windows for Maggie to arrive. The front door to Garrett's house opened almost before Maggie had stepped out of her car. The first thing Maggie noticed was that the girl's face was pale and clammy looking, her fire-orange hair limp and tangled. She wore a pair of red plaid shorts that clashed with her yellow-and-pink-striped T-shirt, both sadly crumpled. Her left arm cradled a placid-looking white cat—not quite full grown, but a little older than kitten stage. Tears had left sticky trails down Kix's cheeks and her lower lip still quivered.

She threw herself at Maggie, wrapping her free arm tightly around Maggie's waist.

Maggie gave the child a reassuring hug even as she asked, "Where are Payton and your dad?"

"Payton's in her bed. Daddy fell asleep on the couch."

"You said your grandmother is sick, too? Is she here?"

Kix shook her head against Maggie's chest. "Meemaw is taking care of her at their house. Meemaw isn't sick, but she can't take care of everybody, so Daddy said we didn't need her here."

Kix didn't feel feverish, to Maggie's relief. "How long has this been going on?"

"I got sick Friday at Grammy's house while Daddy was at work. Grammy took me to the doctor and he said it was a nasty virus that's going around. Then yesterday Payton got sick and then Grammy and this morning Daddy got it. I feel a little better now, but everyone else is sick and I can't take care of them all," she added in a little wail, her eyes filling again.

"That's okay, sweetheart. I can," Maggie assured her.

Kix sniffled and wiped her face with her free hand. "What if you get sick, too?"

"Don't worry about me. I'll be fine. Your new kitty is beautiful, by the way."

The faintest hint of a smile lightened the child's uncharacteristically grave expression. "Her name is Sasha. Daddy likes her because he says she's the most laid-back cat ever. I love her because she likes to be hugged and petted and she sleeps with me and plays with strings and toy mice and she's the best cat in the whole world."

It was good to hear Kix babbling again, even if her voice was still a little unsteady.

"Nice to meet you, Sasha." Maggie scratched one soft, pointed ear, then straightened. "Now let's see what we can do about getting you all well."

Though still clean, the house wasn't quite as militarily tidy as it had been on her previous visit. A stack of unopened mail lay on the foyer table and a pair of girl's sandals—Kix's, apparently—had been abandoned on the floor just inside the door. Kix led her to the living room. A newspaper was tossed on the floor beside an easy chair. A couple more pairs of shoes lay haphazardly on the floor, along with a few scattered cat toys. Two soda cans and an empty dish sat on the coffee table. The television was tuned to a kids' program, the volume turned low, but no one was watching.

Maggie's gaze turned to the couch. More specifically, to the man sprawled on the couch, his head cradled on a pillow, one arm dangling off the side. As her grandfather would say, Garrett looked like he'd been rode hard and put up wet. His eyes were closed, his dark lashes stark against skin pale beneath the tan. His mouth was drawn into a hard line and deep lines creased his damp forehead. His usually neat, short dark hair stood in spikes around his head, either from contact with the pillow or from swipes of his hand. There was a stain on his gray T-shirt and his feet were bare beneath the hems of his faded jeans. He looked so different from the composed, dignified pilot she usually saw—and yet still very much the strong, virile man she'd fallen so hard for.

He roused suddenly, squeezing his forehead with one hand as though his head ached, his voice hoarse when he muttered, "Damn it, I fell asleep. Kix?"

Kix stepped forward. "I'm here, Daddy. And so is Maggie."

He froze, then dropped his hand, rising unsteadily on one elbow. "Maggie?"

She stepped into his line of sight. "Hello, Garrett."

She could almost see him struggling to clear his head. "What are you…? This isn't a good time to visit, Maggie. I'd hate for you to catch what we've got."

"I'm not here to visit. I'm here to help."

"That's very kind of you, but—"

"Yes, I know," she cut in, "you're doing fine on your own. You have everything under control."

"We're getting by."

"Clearly. But now you have help. Go to bed, Garrett. Take some medicine, drink some water and get some sleep. I'll take care of the girls."

He shook his head, then grabbed his forehead again when the movement seemed to make him dizzy. "I can't ask you to—"

"You didn't ask," she reminded him firmly. "Sometimes I just take charge, remember?"

His glittering eyes met hers for a moment. "I remember."

She smiled. "Go to bed, Garrett. You can resist me again later."

Dragging himself to his bare feet, he swayed in place a moment before giving in and heading for the doorway. "I'm beginning to think resistance is futile," he muttered on his way out.

With a little laugh, Maggie looked down at wide-eyed Kix, who now sat cross-legged on the floor with her cat. "Your daddy is a Trekkie?"

Kix gave a little snort. "Big time."

"Interesting."

Anticipating some entertaining debates about which version of the *Trek* universe was the best, Maggie waited until she was sure Garrett had gone to rest before turning to his youngest daughter. "Have you had any lunch?"

Kix shook her head. "Daddy was going to make some soup but then he fell asleep."

Maggie nodded. "I'll check on Payton and then make you some lunch."

"I can help you. I'm feeling a lot better than I was," Kix assured her.

Resting a hand momentarily on the girl's head, Maggie smiled. "I'm glad to hear that. Now, why don't you go wash your face and hands while I check on your sister?"

"Okay, Maggie." Looking a bit more like her usual energetic self, Kix gathered the extraordinarily patient Sasha into her arms and dashed off to comply.

Maggie found Payton's bedroom easily enough. The first door on the right of the back hallway stood open and Payton was asleep in the bed. Tiptoeing across the floor, Maggie made a quick visual sweep of the room, noting the signs of transition between childhood and young adulthood: colorful stuffed animals were arranged on a shelf beneath a poster of a current teen idol. A tube of tinted lip balm and a few plastic bangle bracelets were scattered on the dresser beside a unicorn figurine. A crumpled pair of shorts and a T-shirt lay on the floor beside a tumbled pair of flip-flops adorned with flirty fabric daisies.

Standing beside the bed, Maggie studied the teenager sleeping fretfully on the bunched pillows. She'd kicked off her covers, revealing a thin purple sleep cami and lavender plaid sleep shorts. Even though Payton looked touchingly young and vulnerable in her illness, Maggie still saw the hints of the beautiful, strong-willed woman she would become.

Gently smoothing the mint-green sheets up to Payton's waist, Maggie smiled when she saw that the girl slept with a stuffed toy. At first glance it appeared to be a once-white teddy bear. Upon closer examination, Maggie realized it was a snowman. The body was made of a thick, velvety material stuffed into a squishy trilobe shape. Black buttons served as eyes and the embroidered red mouth wore a permanent smile. A jaunty black felt hat, rather misshapen from years of squashing, and a red knit scarf with somewhat ragged ends were its only garments. From the toy's condition, it was obvious that it had been well loved for quite a few years. Something about the sight of it cradled next to Payton made Maggie smile wistfully even as her throat tightened.

Raising her gaze, she saw that Payton's eyes had opened. They glittered more brightly than usual, perhaps with a touch of fever. Her arms tightened around the toy. "My mom bought it for me when I was little," she croaked. "On a ski trip to Colorado."

Maggie nodded, unsurprised. "You must miss her very much."

Payton's full lower lip quivered just for a moment. "Sometimes."

And this was one of those times, Maggie suspected. Did Payton ever feel free to talk about her loss with her father and grandmother, neither of whom had been part of the home Payton had shared with her mom, at least not that she remembered?

As she emerged a bit more from her heavy sleep, Payton frowned. "Why are you here?"

Maggie couldn't help but be amused by how much Payton suddenly sounded like her father. "I came to help," she said as she had to him.

"Where's my dad?"

"He's not feeling well. He's resting. I was going to make some lunch for Kix. Are you hungry?"

Payton shifted in the bed as if to rise. "I can make something for them. You don't need to stay."

Maggie didn't take offense. "I know I don't need to, but I'd like to, if you don't mind very much. Why don't you rest a little longer and I'll go make some lunch. I'll see if you're hungry when it's done."

Subsiding into the pillows again, Payton shifted her obviously aching head restlessly as if in search of a more comfortable position. "Whatever."

Leaving the door open behind her, Maggie quietly left the bedroom and headed for the kitchen where Kix waited for her.

Twenty minutes later a hearty pot of soup simmered on the stove. In deference to the hot summer day, Maggie had kept the soup light—a chicken broth base with finely chopped fresh veggies and a handful of rotini, ingredients she'd found in Garrett's well-stocked pantry. She ladled soup into bowls and set out crackers and cheese while Kix filled tumblers with ice and water. She didn't prepare a bowl for Garrett; from what she'd seen of him, he needed sleep more than food at the moment.

Payton's eyes were closed when Maggie entered her room, but she roused as Maggie approached the bed. "Is Dad still asleep?"

"Yes. Are you hungry? I've made some soup."

Payton hesitated only a moment before nodding. "I'm a little hungry."

"Do you want me to bring you a tray or do you feel like eating in the kitchen?"

Setting her grinning snowman aside, Payton pushed herself upright and swung her legs to the side of the bed. "I'll get up. I'm tired of being in bed."

Lingering only long enough to make sure the girl was steady on her feet, Maggie moved toward the doorway. "The soup will be ready for you when you've washed up."

Maggie had just settled Kix at the table with her lunch when Payton joined them a few minutes later.

She had made a haphazard attempt to comb her hair and had swapped her sleep clothes for clean shorts and a tee, though she'd left her feet bare. She was still pale and there were faint purple shadows beneath her heavy-lidded eyes, but she held her chin high and walked steadily toward her place at the table.

"I helped Maggie make the soup," Kix boasted as Payton picked up her spoon. "It's really good."

Payton took a cautious bite, then nodded somewhat grudgingly. "It is good."

Maggie smiled at her and pushed the cheese-and-cracker tray a little closer.

After taking another bite of soup and a sip of her water, Payton asked, "Did Dad call you?"

Kix shook her head. "I called her," she admitted. "I found her number in Daddy's phone. I knew she'd want to come help us."

"Why would she want to come take care of sick people?" Payton scoffed.

"Because these sick people are very important to her," Maggie replied evenly. "I'm glad Kix called."

Leaving the girls to eat, Maggie filled an insulated container with a good portion of the big pot of soup and carried it across the street to Garrett's mother and grandmother. She'd called earlier to check on them, learning that Paulette was feeling somewhat better and that Esther had somehow escaped catching the virus so far. They seemed to appreciate the soup and the knowledge that Garrett and the girls had someone to help them for a few hours. If they read anything meaningful into Kix calling Maggie, or Maggie dropping everything to respond, they kept their speculation to themselves. Maggie made them promise to call if they needed anything before she returned to Garrett's house.

After clearing the kitchen, she joined the girls in the living room to watch a movie from their video library. Maggie sat in the center of the couch with Kix curled beside her, holding her dozing cat. After a few minutes, Payton settled on her other side. "I can see the TV better from here," she said gruffly.

Maggie merely nodded and shifted her position to better accommodate both girls.

Kix leaned drowsily against Maggie's right shoulder. Though her eyes were focused on the screen, her attention seemed to be wandering. "I'm glad you're here, Maggie," she said. They had the sound from the film turned rather low so she didn't have to raise her voice to be heard.

Wrapping her right arm around the girl's warm little body, Maggie rested her cheek for a moment against the top of Kix's head. "So am I, sweetie."

"I hope Dad will at least be in a better mood now that you're here," Payton muttered from her other side.

Maggie turned her head with a slight frown. "He isn't still cross with you, is he?"

It had been more than a week since Payton's escapade in the boat and while Maggie wouldn't expect Garrett to just forget about the scare Payton had given them, she wouldn't have thought he would stretch out the punishment this long. That seemed a bit excessive.

"He hasn't really been cross," Payton conceded. "Just kind of quiet."

"Sad," Kix said with one of her moments of oddly mature insight. "He's been a little sad since we left the resort. Payton thought it was because he was disappointed with her, but I said I thought he missed you."

Maggie wasn't sure what to say in response to that.

"I don't like Daddy being sad," Kix said somberly.

"Neither do I," Payton whispered.

"I think we can all agree that we don't want your father to be sad," Maggie assured them.

"Did you and Daddy have a fight, Maggie?" Kix asked then, her tone hesitant.

"No, sweetie, we didn't have a fight."

"Then why haven't we seen you since we left?"

"Because of us, stupid," Payton snapped crossly, rubbing her temples with both hands. "Do you really think she wants to hang around with us all the time, especially when I…"

"When you what, Payton?" Maggie urged gently.

Her voice thick now, Payton ducked her head as she answered, "When I do stupid stuff and get in trouble with Dad. And I don't even know why."

Shifting again on the couch, Maggie muted the television and wrapped her left arm around Payton. The girl stiffened a bit, but didn't try to pull away. "Because you're thirteen, honey. We all do foolish things when we're thirteen and trying to grow up too fast. I did, too."

She wouldn't tell the girls all the crazy stunts she got into at that age—usually trying to keep up with her cousin Steven—because she certainly didn't want either Payton or Kix trying to imitate them, but she wanted them to know she understood. "As for wanting to spend time with you and Kix, I love being with you both. Your dad and I have some adult issues to work out between us, but whatever happens there, the three of us—me and you, Payton, and you, too, Kix—will always be friends. At least, I hope you both consider me your friend. No one will ever replace your mom, but there's always room in your life for another good friend, right?"

"You're *my* friend, Maggie," Kix said eagerly.

Maggie dropped a kiss on the girl's head. "Thank you, sweetie."

She glanced then at Payton, holding her breath while the older sister considered the situation. And then Payton nodded. "I want to be your friend, too. Even though I think sometimes you're going to agree with Dad instead of me."

Even to herself, Maggie's chuckle sounded a little shaky. "Maybe sometimes. Once you get to be my age, you'll find yourself getting overprotective about people you love, too."

Payton blinked a few times, then nodded in acceptance. "My head hurts," she murmured.

"Would you like to go lie down again?"

The girl shook her head and slowly relaxed into Maggie's encircling arm. "No. Could we just stay right here for a while?"

"Of course." Snuggled on the couch with both girls, Maggie nodded toward the silenced television. "Do you want me to turn the sound on again?"

"Could we just talk?" Payton asked, her head on Maggie's shoulder.

"Absolutely. What would you like to talk about?"

Kix scooted down on the couch, her head in Maggie's lap, her eyelids looking a little heavy, one hand absently stroking her pet. "Let Payton choose. I'm kind of tired."

Maggie stroked the child's hair, thinking Kix must still be a little sick if she was too tired to chatter. At least her little face felt cool, if a bit clammy.

Payton spoke quietly. "I don't care. Anything."

Drawing a deep breath, Maggie suggested, "Why don't you tell me about your mom? What sort of things did the three of you like to do together?"

After a long hesitation, Payton began to talk, the

words escaping her as if they'd been pent up much too long. Kix contributed sleepily to the conversation a few times, but Payton did most of the talking, sharing the memories she treasured most of her outgoing, active, ambitious but obviously loving mother. Maggie asked an occasional question, but mostly just listened, forming a new image of the woman she'd heard about before only from the ex-husband. Someone should have initiated this conversation with the girls months ago, she thought. Or maybe they were only now ready to talk about their loss. Whatever the case, she was glad to be here now to offer an encouraging ear to her young friends.

Soon she would need to have an extensive conversation with Garrett. She wasn't sure how he would react to having her here, so deeply involved in his daughters' lives. But she would worry about that later, she thought, nestling a little more comfortably with his drowsy girls.

Garrett opened his eyes to darkness. It took a few moments for his vision to adjust enough for him to see that he lay in his own bed. Automatically he glanced at the bedside clock. The numbers he saw glowing there brought him straight upright with a gasp. How could it be 10:00 p.m.? The last clear thought he remembered was that he needed to make lunch for the girls, as soon as he'd rested for a few minutes on the couch.

Maggie. Did he really remember Maggie coming into his house, ordering him to bed? Or was that just a weird dream, one of many involving her since he'd left the resort more than a week ago?

And where were his girls? Why was the house so quiet? Throwing his legs off the side of the bed, he stood, stumbled, quickly regained his balance and headed for the doorway.

The doors to their bedrooms were ajar, the rooms inside dark and quiet. Still, both girls kept nightlights burning in their rooms, providing enough illumination for him to see that they were in their beds, sound asleep. He padded to each bedside to make sure. Both felt blessedly cool to his light touch and seemed to be sleeping comfortably. The cat sleeping next to Kix meowed when he disturbed it, but Garrett quieted it with a quick pat. Considering how miserable the past couple of nights had been for all of them, he didn't want to risk waking either of his daughters.

Suddenly almost unbearably thirsty, he moved toward the kitchen. A light in the living room distracted him and he veered in that direction. If Maggie really had been here earlier, surely she had left by now?

He found her sitting on the couch. Her legs were pulled up in front of her while she watched an old *Star Trek: The Next Generation* episode on the quietly modulated television and simultaneously checked the screen of her smartphone as if reading texts or status updates. A half-empty glass of iced tea sat on a coaster beside her and a half-eaten brownie lay on a plate next to it. She looked perfectly at home in his living room. As if she belonged just there.

Shaking his head to clear his mind of such dangerous thoughts, he asked, "Why are you here?"

She looked up with an amused smile that made his breath catch in his throat. "That's the second time you've asked me that. Good evening to you, too."

He was still having a little trouble thinking clearly. "Did you answer me when I asked before?"

"I told you I was here to help. You needed me," she said simply.

He wondered if she had any idea how true that was.

The thought made his voice gruff when he asked, "How did you know to come? Surely my mother didn't call—"

"Kix called me," she surprised him by saying. And then she shook a finger at him. "I forbid you to fuss at her about it. I'm glad she called me. Of course I wanted to help."

He frowned as he made another massive attempt to clear his head. "How long was I out?"

She glanced at the clock on her phone screen. "Nine hours, give or take a little. It was just after one when I arrived. I made soup for the girls for lunch, carried some over to your mom and grandmother and then ordered pizza for dinner. Not the healthiest choice, I know, but the girls requested it and your mom and grandmother looked pleased when I took one to them. Kix told me your grandmother loves pizza. I tucked the girls into their beds a little while ago because they were both still so tired from their illness and they both went straight to sleep."

She'd fed his family—his entire family—soup and pizza while he'd slept like a lump in the same house. "I'm sorry you went to so much trouble," he said stiffly, pushing a hand through his disheveled hair. "I can't believe I went out like that. The girls—"

"—were fine," she completed for him firmly. "At some level, I'm sure you knew I was taking care of them or you wouldn't have been able to rest so well. They told me you've hardly had any sleep at all for the past couple of nights while you were sitting with them and your mother. Being sick yourself, you needed the rest. I checked on you a couple of times to see if you needed anything, but you were obviously exhausted, so I thought sleep was the best medicine for you."

The thought of her looking down at him as he'd slept

made him even more uncomfortable than the image of her making soup in his kitchen. What must she be thinking of him now?

"I could have handled it."

Still smiling gently, she set her phone aside and stood. "You were handling everything fine. As I said, I'm sure you'd have stayed awake today if you'd thought you needed to do so for the girls, but you knew they were okay. That you could trust me with them."

"Of course I trust you with them. That's not the point—"

She gave a little shrug, her expression hard to read. "Maybe I was the one who lacked faith in myself. I wasn't sure I could give them what they needed. Wasn't sure I even wanted to try," she admitted with typical candor. "But you know? Now I think maybe I'm exactly what this family needs."

He drew a deep, sharp breath. "I think I need something to drink."

Maybe dehydration was clouding his mind, making him read meaning into her words that couldn't possibly be right. If he wasn't careful, he was going to start babbling, telling her how much he'd missed her, how many times he'd reached for her in the night, how often he'd started to call her just to hear her voice before he came to his senses and set down the phone. He'd told himself repeatedly that there was no future for them for so many reasons. That there was no need to continue something that could only lead to disappointment and heartache. He'd gotten involved before with the wrong woman and it had been a disaster. And while Maggie was very, very different from Breanne, that didn't mean she was any more right for him.

But damn, he'd missed her. As much as he'd once

thought he loved Breanne, he'd never felt quite like this with her.

"Come into the kitchen," Maggie said, placing a hand on his arm. "There's more of the soup I made for lunch. It's very good soup, if I do say so myself. My grandmother's recipe—though I didn't mention that to *your* grandmother when I served her some of it. You'll feel much better after you've had something to eat."

"You should go," he said abruptly, because he wanted so much to let her lead him anywhere she wanted to take him. To feed him soup and tuck him into bed—and then to climb in with him. The very strength of that longing made him repeat hoarsely, "You should go."

Frowning a little, she raised a hand to his forehead. "Do you have fever? Maybe you should take something. You're not making much sense."

Her touch sent a flash of electricity from his head to his groin. He caught her wrist to pull her hand away, but then didn't want to let her go. "It can't work, Maggie. I have my girls and my job. My mom and grandmother. There's no time left. Breanne said I was boring, that I didn't have time for fun with her because I was always so busy doing for everyone else. She was right. I have no more extra time for you."

"You do have fever," Maggie fretted as if she hadn't heard a word he'd said. "Come into the kitchen, I'll warm some soup and find something for your fever. You'll feel a lot better afterward."

"You aren't—" He sighed when he found himself talking to her back as she walked away from him. Following because he had no other choice, he waited until they'd reached the kitchen before trying again. "You aren't listening to me."

She'd already pulled a covered bowl from the refrigerator. "I'm listening," she said as she turned toward the microwave. "I'm just not taking you seriously. You're obviously feverish. A little fuzzy-headed. We'll talk more when you feel better."

"Damn it, Maggie, you can't just come into my house and take charge as if…as if you belong here."

Pushing buttons on the microwave, she said without turning to look at him, "You keep talking like that and I'll think you don't want me here."

His hands clenched involuntarily into fists. "What makes you think that's not the truth?"

Her smile tremulous, she turned to face him then, a spoon and napkin held in a white-knuckled grip that belied her easy tone. "Because I know you pretty well by now, no matter how hard you've tried to hold me at a distance. And because you've been sad. I've been sad, too, Garrett. I've missed you."

"Why—" His voice lodged in his dry throat. Impatiently, he filled a glass with water, downed half of it, then set it down with a thump. "Why do you think I've been sad?"

"I have my sources," she murmured, making him wonder exactly what his daughters had told her. "Were they right? Have you missed me, Garrett?"

He should tell her no, of course. Tell her he'd been getting along just fine. That his life was plenty full with his family and his business, that there were no gaping holes that only she could fill. All of which would be a blatant lie. "I've missed you," he said roughly. "I've missed you so damned much. Which doesn't mean—"

Her fingertips fell lightly over his lips, and her smile was almost blinding. "That's all I wanted to hear. Eat your soup, Garrett, and then take your medicine. Let someone else take care of you for a change. When's the last time anyone did that?"

He honestly couldn't remember. Probably since he'd graduated from high school and left his mother's house to join the military.

Too tired to argue with her any longer—for now—he let her push him into a chair and set soup and ibuprofen in front of him. He dutifully downed the medicine, then took a bite of the soup, which was as good as she'd immodestly boasted. Almost before he knew it, he'd eaten the whole bowlful and drunk another glass of water while Maggie fussed around him.

"I'm spending the night," she mentioned when she collected his empty bowl to stack in the dishwasher.

He choked on the last sip of his water.

"I won't stay in your room, of course," she added lightly. "I don't think that would set a good example for the girls. I found the guest room earlier, so I'll stay in there tonight, just to make sure everyone gets plenty of sleep. I'll head back to the resort after I make breakfast for everyone. I'll check on your mom in the morning, too, though she said she was feeling much better when I took the pizza over to her."

She ran a hand over his hair as if to smooth it, a comfortable, affectionate gesture that made his throat ache again. "Maybe when everyone's feeling better, you and I can get a few hours away to ourselves. I don't know about you, but I could use some us time. As busy and responsible as you are, I'm sure you can find a couple hours occasionally for that."

"Us time?"

She smiled and nodded. "I like the sound of it, don't you?"

"Yes." He swallowed. "I like it very much."

She leaned down to kiss his cheek. "No offense, but you're not getting any kisses on the lips until you're fever-free. As much as I want to share your life with you, you can just keep this virus all to yourself."

He might have been amused by the quip if his head wasn't still spinning in a way that had nothing to do with the virus and everything to do with Maggie.

"I'm in love with you, Maggie." The words escaped him before he could stop them. Maybe later he would blame the fever.

She sighed gustily. "Well, darn."

He blinked, then frowned. Her response wasn't exactly what he'd expected, considering the broad hints he thought she had been dropping.

She cupped his face between her hands. "I love you, too, Garrett McHale. And if I catch your virus, you'd damned well better make me soup."

She planted her lips firmly on his before he had a chance to promise her he'd make her anything she wanted.

It was almost two weeks later when Maggie and Garrett finally found a chance to slip away for significant us time. His two sick days following only a week after his family vacation had put him quite a bit behind at work, and the busy summer season kept Maggie hopping at the resort, leaving them few stolen hours to spend together. But the last Saturday evening in July found them alone in a luxurious Dallas hotel suite, snuggled together in a bed that looked almost the size of Maggie's bedroom in her mobile home.

They'd left the girls with Garrett's mother and grandmother for the weekend, giving Garrett and Maggie almost two whole days to spend together. They'd spent the whole day in Dallas, shopping and visiting museums and dining on steak and seafood for dinner, holding hands and kissing and talking about nothing of any significance. It had been glorious, and they had almost all day tomorrow to repeat the indulgent behavior. But first they had tonight, she thought, snuggling happily into his strong arms. All night.

Her cheek rested against his bare chest and she could feel his heart still beating quickly from their first round of energetic lovemaking. Her own pulse still raced happily. She sighed in contentment. "What a perfect day."

She felt him drop a kiss on the top of her head. "It was," he agreed.

Trailing a fingertip down the center of his chest toward the sheet that covered him below the waist, she murmured, "It's not quite over yet."

Garrett chuckled and caught her hand. "Give me a couple of minutes to recover. Remember, I'm not as young as you are."

She laughed and propped her chin on her hands to look at him. "I'd say you more than keep up."

"I'll take that as a compliment. I guess."

"It was intended as one."

Smoothing a strand of hair from her cheek, he asked idly, "What do you want to do tomorrow?"

"Anything. Everything," she said. "I'm just loving this time alone together."

He smiled, but his eyes had gone suddenly grave. She studied him closely, wondering what he was thinking now.

"Maybe I can schedule more weekends like this," he suggested. "Just the two of us, I mean. If not a whole weekend, perhaps we could arrange a night here and there."

"I hope we can get away occasionally, but I understand that you have a lot of obligations at home. We both do. We've been coordinating our schedules pretty well, I think, getting dinner together most evenings and time together on weekends."

"Well, yeah, but that's usually with family around. This is the first chance we've had to be alone—and you said it's been perfect."

"And it has been. Which doesn't mean I don't appreciate the time we spend with our families."

He sighed, sounding suddenly impatient. "What I'm trying to say is, I don't expect you to spend every spare minute away from work with me and the kids. I know you have friends, a busy social life—"

She understood suddenly where this was leading. "You think I'm bored spending time with you and the kids? You're wrong. I love those girls. Now that Payton has realized I'm more interested in being her friend than another authority figure in her life, we're getting along very well—though I'm not so naive as to think we'll never have a quarrel or disagreement in the future.

"I'll still see my friends when I want to," she continued before he could say anything else, "and I'm sure I'll have other things I'll want to do occasionally, just as I expect you will. But that busy social life you mentioned? For the most part, it was just stuff to do when I wasn't in the mood to stay home alone and read or sew. Now I'm very happy being with you and the girls."

"And we love having you with us," he assured her, his sincerity evident in his tone. "But I remember a time when you suggested that you and I could get together away from the kids, keeping our relationship just between us."

She grimaced. "I was an idiot, wasn't I? To think

we could have any sort of relationship that didn't include your girls. Or that I would even want a relationship like that. Your kids are the most important part of your life, and I can't imagine you without them. I've accepted that loving you means loving them, too, and I wouldn't have it any other way."

He shifted so that she was on her back with him leaning over her, one hand on her face. "You know how afraid I was to let you into my life. I worried that we'd mess this up—or maybe that I would mess it up—and the girls would be hurt again. Or that I'd do something stupid and hurt you. Hell, I worried about getting hurt again myself."

Her smile was soft. "That's understandable. It couldn't have been easy for you to admit defeat in your marriage."

"It wasn't. But it was obvious that it wasn't working. That I couldn't make her happy."

"It wasn't your responsibility to make her happy," she murmured, rubbing a hand up and down his arm. "You didn't fail, Garrett. You were just unsuited to each other."

"I guess."

"By the way, there's something I've been meaning to say about Breanne. I'm sure she was a good woman and a brilliant attorney and a fine mother to your girls—but she was very wrong about one thing." She reached up to touch the face of the man she loved—the sexy pilot, the ex-military officer, the talented musician, the dutiful son and grandson, the dedicated father, the thrilling lover. She would not change one thing about him, even if she could.

Catching her hand, Garrett pressed a kiss into her

palm, a flick of his tongue making her shiver in pleasure. "What's that?"

Tangling her legs with his, she drew him down onto her. "You are so not boring."

His husky chuckle sounded pleased before she smothered it with her mouth.

Epilogue

The wedding took place on a pleasantly mild Sunday afternoon in September. The Bell Resort pavilion had been bedecked with green garlands and white blossoms, with gold-trimmed white bows and filmy white tulle. The bride wore a simple white sheath dress and flowers in her hair, while the groom wore a dark suit and a satisfied smile. Hannah served as her sister's matron of honor. Because Garrett's best friend was performing the ceremony, Garrett had asked an old friend from his military days to stand as best man. Dressed in white-and-pink ruffles, Kix made a charming flower girl, and Payton had selected a pretty white lace dress for her role as ring bearer, giving them both an important task for the ceremony.

The Bell and McHale families sat in folding chairs beneath the pavilion, not separated into bride's side and groom's side, but mingled into a united group. Their grandmothers occupied places of honor at the front where they could clearly see every detail of the simple but beautiful wedding. Occasionally their eyes met during the ceremony that formally connected their two families, and they shared faint, rather bemused smiles.

Jay's voice had just a little catch when he concluded the ceremony and invited the happy couple to exchange their first married kiss. More than a few tears were blotted as the tall, handsome pilot tenderly kissed his glowing bride. And standing off to one side, the groom's two daughters grinned at each other and shared a smug, surreptitious high five.

* * * * *

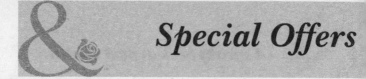
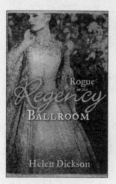

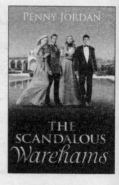